Deep down in the metal heart of the great Traction City of London, a ruthless killer is at work. The glowing green eyes of something not at all human glimmer in the rusting darkness of the Base Tier. Three men lie dead, and each one is missing a hand…

A spine-chilling story from the sensational future world of Mortal Engines.

This book has been specially written and published for World Book Day 2011. For further information please see www.worldbookday.com.

World Book Day in the UK and Ireland is made possible by generous sponsorship from National Book Tokens, participating publishers, authors and booksellers. Booksellers who accept the £1 World Book Day Token bear the full cost of redeeming it.

THE WORLD OF
MORTAL ENGINES

TRACTION CITY

Philip Reeve

PHILIP REEVE

With illustrations by the author

SCHOLASTIC

For Jeremy Levett, who lent a hand

First published in the UK in 2011 by Scholastic Children's Books
An imprint of Scholastic Ltd
Euston House, 24 Eversholt Street
London, NW1 1DB, UK
Registered office: Westfield Road, Southam, Warwickshire, CV47 0RA
SCHOLASTIC and associated logos are trademarks and/or registered
trademarks of Scholastic Inc.

ISBN 9781407124278

Printed in Great Britain by Clays Ltd, St Ives Plc, Bungay, Suffolk.
Papers used by Scholastic Children's Books
are made from wood grown in sustainable forests.

1 3 5 7 9 10 8 6 4 2

This is a work of fiction. Names, characters, places, incidents and
dialogues are products of the author's imagination or are used fictitiously.
Any resemblance to actual people, living or dead, events or locales is
entirely coincidental.

www.scholastic.co.uk/zone

1

These were mountains once. In Ancient times men knew them as the Alps. But bad things have happened to them in the centuries since: earthstorms and ice ages; a Slow Bomb strike in the Sixty Minute War. Now they are the Shattercountry, a steep land of rubble riven by clefts and rat-runs where the mining towns crawl, gnawing ore out of stumps that once were mighty peaks.

But tonight the passes are deserted. The mining towns have fled. The Shatterlands shiver at the coming of a new disaster. Up from the lowlands, engines roaring, smokestacks spewing thunderheads, a city is advancing. Banks of gigantic caterpillar tracks grind the ground to gravel as it goes. Above them, stacked in seven tiers like the layers of a wedding cake, the body of the city towers; factories and work-yards on the largest, lowest level, shops and houses on the ones above. The higher tiers are smaller and have parks about their edges, though the wild winds of the Shatterlands have stripped the trees of leaves. On the tiny topmost tier, among the council offices and politicians' palaces, an ancient temple to a forgotten god has been rebuilt, in honour of the city's past. Even the wretched Anti-Tractionists, watching from their hilltop hovels as it lumbers by, know the famous dome of St Paul's Cathedral. It tells them that this juggernaut is not just any city; this is London, first and greatest of all the Traction Cities of the earth.

For centuries now it has dominated the Great Hunting Ground that lies north of here, devouring smaller, slower towns to feed its endless need for fuel and raw material. Now, for the first time, its ruling council has decided to take it across the high passes to hunt upon the plains of Italia.

Smiff, ten years old and creeping catlike through the city's bowels, knows none of this. The Council might as well be gods to him, they live so high above the dank and rusty streets he knows. On the bits of Base Tier where he makes his living there are some worrying-looking rust holes in the deck plates, and you can look down through them sometimes and see the great wheels turning and the ground sliding by far below. But Smiff never knows which bit of ground it is, or what part of the wide world his city is hunting in. All he knows this evening is that London is climbing, and has been climbing for a long while. The roar from the engines is louder and harsher than usual; streets that are usually flat have developed a steep slope; the heat is immense.

One good thing about living in the chassis of a Traction City is this: the stuff that rich folk drop on tiers above comes down to you. Maybe a lady on Tier One feels the clasp of her necklace break while she's taking the air in Circle Park. Before she can stop it it's slithered through one of the gratings in the deck that lets light and air down to the tier below. It lands in the busy streets of Bloomsbury, where the wheels of one of those new electric cars clip it and send it down another grating to Tier Three. And slowly, if Smiff's lucky and no sharp-eyed Smiff-like person on the higher levels spots it, the ceaseless movements of the city shake it down from level to level, through grating after grating, until lands at last where all things must, on the grimy deck plates of Base Tier.

At least, that's what Smiff is hoping as he scurries towards Mortlake this evening. It's been a long time since he found anything better than a bent fork, but there are good gratings in the roof of Mortlake, aligned with other gratings right up through the city. All sorts of strange stuff comes rattling down to Mortlake.

Mortlake is an old industrial section, part of a huge complex called the Wombs, where, back in the glory days, London used to build whole suburbs for itself, refitting towns it caught and sending them off covered in bunting and civic pride, carrying some of London's excess population away with them. But it's been sixty years since the last suburb was launched, and Mortlake has fallen into disuse. DANGER – KEEP OUT say signs on the chain-link fences which bar all the approaches. Smiff's spent his life ignoring signs like that.

He looks left, then right, checking that no coppers are lurking. Then it's over the fence as easy as a monkey and down again into Mortlake's corroded gloom.

No lights here. No names above the rusty shopfronts. Fly-posters pasted to the huge support pillars advertise shows and patent cure-alls from fifty years ago. The district's few narrow streets wind around the flanks of the three colossal hangars in which suburbs were once built. In places where daylight can reach, wan clumps of nettles sprout among the rust flakes on the deck.

Smiff takes out his home-made torch and shines it on the deck ahead. He plays it over the heaps of debris that have collected against forward-facing walls as the city climbs, looking for shiny stuff that might have trickled down from tiers above.

In the first pile he searches there's a pewter button. Not much, but better than nothing, Smiff thinks (which is actually quite a good description of his whole life). He pockets it and moves on.

In the second pile there's just a fish head; shiny enough, but worthless, even to Smiff.

As he turns away the beam of his torch lights up the steel toecaps of a pair of boots.

Smiff raises the torch, and his eyes. Above the boots are trousers. Above the trousers, a paisley waistcoat. Inside the waistcoat a big, broad, red-faced man. Behind the man, two more, much like him.

"This here is *my* patch, kid," says Costa Mulligan, king of the Base Tier scavs.

"I'm sorry, Mister M," says Smiff, already sure that "sorry" won't be good enough. He looks past the men for an escape route. There's a rust hole in the deck plate there. If he could drop through that he'd land in the nets under the city. Provided the nets are strong enough to hold him. Provided Mulligan's boys haven't stripped them away to sell. He gauges the distance, wondering if he can make it to the hole before they grab him.

Turns out he can't. The men step forward and lift him, one by either arm. Mulligan grins down at him. A knife appears. The Life of Smiff seems destined to have a sudden and disappointing end. Until, surprising as a whirlwind, something comes out of the dark between the boarded-up buildings on the right. There is a scream. One of the men who was holding Smiff lets go. Then the other. Something reaches over his head for Mulligan. Smiff doesn't wait to find out what it is. He's gone, running for that rust hole and jumping through it, down into the wind beneath the city, the sudden, shocking cold of open air.

Nets of metal mesh are strung across the gulfs between London's banks of caterpillar tracks.

6

They are meant to save hapless workers who tumble off the city's underside while they are repairing it. They are rusty, and in places parts are missing altogether, but Smiff's luck holds; the net beneath the rust hole is sound, and he doesn't weigh much; he crashes down on it and lies there winded. All around him the chill wind whinnies, and the dark is full of the *scherlink, scherlink, scherlink* of the huge treads passing, the grumble of the wheels, the squeal and grind of axles. But Smiff's not listening to any of those noises. He's still hearing the sounds from above; the awful sobbing screams which cut off suddenly and leave a silence which is worse. The heavy footfalls, as if (he thinks) some statue's sprung to life and is pacing about up there.

Something drops on him through the rust hole and he sees it falling just in time and rolls aside so that it doesn't crush him. It lands in the nets next to him, slack and weighty, unmoving till the movement of London sets it swinging. Smiff fumbles his torch on.

The slack and weighty thing is Costa Mulligan, or was till recently. Where his throat was there is now only red. And as Smiff drops his precious torch and goes scrambling for his life towards safer districts of the city he has time to notice one more nasty detail. The man's right hand is missing; severed at the wrist.

2

London climbs higher and higher as the night draws on. The last steep ridge of the Shatterlands looms ahead, swaddled in cloud. Even the auxiliary engines have come on stream now, bellowing with the effort as they help to heave the city up this final slope.

On the edge of Base Tier, snow blows in between the tier supports, melting as it settles on the warm iron pavements. Airdock Green Police Station is quiet tonight, but then most nights are quiet at Airdock Green. Sometimes there's a drunk from the pubs on Crumb Street to deal with, sometimes a pickpocket works the crowds of engine labourers around the elevator station on payday, but by and large there's not much crime down here on Base Tier. It was different in the days when the Airdocks were busy, but there's a smart new air-harbour on Tier Four now where most of the traffic pulls in. The coppers up there must see some cases, Sergeant Anders thinks wistfully as he strolls towards Airdock Green to start his shift. Stolen airships, smugglers, brawls. . . The quays behind his little station are half abandoned, except for some Goshawk 51s which the Guild of Engineers keeps moored there, their plump white envelopes like the speech bubbles of cartoon characters with nothing left to say. Tonight a little shabby red job has joined them; probably some country ship out of the Shatterlands come to shelter from the gale. It's so small that there can barely be room for a single aviator in its gondola. No hope there of a gang of liquored-up sky-boys to add some interest to a policeman's life.

Karl Anders has been thirty years a policeman, but only three of them aboard London. Before that he was chief of police on a little town called Hammershoi, just three tiers tall, that roved around the north country, right up into the Frost

Barrens in the arctic summertime, stopping to trade with other towns it met. A happy place, till one bleak February Thursday it met London, hunting in the north. Anders still misses his quaint old police station; the parks on Obertier, the wooden cupolas of the Temple of Peripatetia – but Hammershoi's engines were just cheap gimcrack copies of the great inventions which drove London. The chase lasted fifteen minutes before London's jaws closed on Hammershoi's chassis and the town was hoiked into London's gut, looted and broken up to feed the hungry city.

There are worse cities to be eaten by. At least London doesn't enslave the people of the towns it eats. They are free to leave if they can think of anywhere to go, or welcome to stay aboard if they wish, and become Londoners as so many have before. So Anders stayed, using his long experience as chief of police to get a job with the London force, the "Coppertops", or "Coppers", as they're called. But they didn't need a chief of police, and refugees from eaten towns aren't welcome on the higher tiers or in high-ranking jobs. So Karl Anders had to start at the bottom again; Base Tier, at the bottom of London, a lowly sergeant, running the quietest cop shop in the city.

He buttons the collar of his blue uniform and pushes open the door, stepping into the hard, flickery light from the electric bulbs in their big tin shades that swing from the ceiling as the city moves. Constable Pym has his feet on the office desk and his nose in a book, but he pulls himself smartly to attention and salutes when Anders enters. A keen lad, just three weeks out of school. In twenty years or so, thinks Anders, he might make a decent policeman.

"Good evening, Pym," he says, in his careful English. "Anything to report, or shall I put on the kettle?"

Pym does have

11

something to report. He can barely keep himself from blurting it out before his sergeant's finished speaking. "Corporal Nutter's got a prisoner, sir!"

Anders puts the kettle on anyway, clamping it carefully into the special fitting on the stove which will keep it there however steeply London tilts. He strikes a match and lights the gas. "What's this prisoner charged with, Constable Pym?"

"Anti-Tractionism, sir," says Corporal Nutter, coming out of the holding cell at the back of the station and closing the door firmly. "Some foreign vermin, come in on a tramp airship, looking to blow us all up. I caught her snooping round the Engine District."

Anders leaves the kettle to boil and goes to the cell door. The peephole on the door lost its cover long ago. He peeps through. A young woman is sitting on the bench at the back of the cell. Not really a woman, just a girl, or at that in-between stage, the age Anders's daughter would have been if she had lived. Only this girl is an easterner: golden skin, black eyes the shape of seeds. Black hair with a startling streak of white in it. Anders guesses at once why Archie Nutter, with his mean, dim-witted, London-for-Londoners prejudices, chose to harass her. She's pretty, too, which maybe didn't help. But what on earth could he have found on her that made him think it worth handcuffing her and bringing her in? Did he stop to consider how much paperwork he'd cause?

He unlocks the cell door with a key from the ring on his belt, unlocks the handcuffs with another. The girl doesn't say anything; just sits there with her long skinny legs stuck out in front of her and her hands resting together on her lap as if they're still cuffed. Anders stands looking at her. Pym and Nutter watch him from the doorway.

"So she's a saboteur, you say?" asks Anders. "Where is your evidence, Corporal Nutter?"

"Here, sir." Nutter passes him a shabby knapsack. It's heavy. Anders looks inside. Whistles softly. He doesn't like to admit it but it seems Archie Nutter may be right, for once.

The thing in the bag is a demolition charge. A silvery disk, like a metal chocolate box or the lid of a tiny manhole. Cities which don't have London's vast Dismantling Yards use them to break up the towns they catch. Attach them to a weak point on the hull, turn that switch to start the timer, stand well back and *boom*. Use a few hundred and and there's no more town, just chunks of useful scrap. But there's no point anywhere on London's hull so weak that a charge *this* small could harm it.

"Are there more of these?" he asks. "You've searched her ship, I assume?"

"I did, sir!" says Constable Pym. Pym has a new boy's respect for paperwork; he hands his sergeant a form headed "*Aerial Merchant Vessel* Jenny Haniver, *Contents and Cargo*". There's not much. Some third-rate jade, a bundle of books, her clothes. No more explosives.

Anders turns back to the girl, still holding the demolition charge. "What were you planning to do with this?"

The girl just stares at him. Her eyes look older than her face. Narrow, black eyes with hurt and hate in them. London shudders, scrambling over boulders almost as big as itself, and the bare bulb on the cell ceiling swings, sloshing shadows over her.

"She don't speak Anglish," says Nutter.

Anders ignores him and squats down in front of the girl, holding the demolition charge with both hands. "Seems to me that maybe there's a simple explanation for this. Like maybe you were hoping to sell this to our demolition crews, not knowing that they have to get all their explosives through the proper channels. If that's so, you should tell me. Because if you don't I'll have to call upstairs. The Guild of Engineers are responsible for dealing with Anti-Tractionists. Once we hand you over to them, I won't be able to help you. So talk to me."

The girl says nothing.

Anders tries not to think about the things the Guild's interrogators will do to her. He tries to think instead about how catching a saboteur will help his career. Maybe there will be a captaincy in it for him. Maybe a better posting, up on one of the higher tiers. He shoos Pym and Nutter from the cell, locks the door, and starts writing a report to send up the pneumatic-tube system to the Engineerium.

He is just folding it ready to put it in the message cylinder when the street door crashes open and a small, ragged figure comes dashing in. Constable Pym catches the boy as he stumbles. He's been running so hard that he can barely breathe, let alone speak. The three policemen gather round him, waiting as he gasps and pants.

"Smiff?" says Constable Pym. "It's Smiff, ain't it? What's the matter?"

"Mull . . . Mull . . . Mulligan. . ." the boy blurts.

"Mulligan's after you?" guesses Anders. "Great Goddess, boy, I've told you children a hundred times not to go scavenging in Mortlake. Has he hurt you?"

"No. . ." The boy looks up at him. In his time as sergeant here Anders has never seen anything but contempt in the eyes of these London scavenger kids. Now he sees fear.

"He's *dead. Murdered.* . ."

3

Sergeant Anders has a key to the fence around Mortlake, though it takes him a while to find it. The Base Tier police don't have the manpower to patrol the empty districts. The council claim they can't afford it, although they always seem to find the funds to pay for policemen on the higher tiers to guard the elevator stops and stairways and make sure no ne'er-do-wells from down below come up to make High London look untidy. Districts like Mortlake are left to police themselves, and so, despite Anders's best efforts, they have fallen into the power of men like Costa Mulligan.

"It'll be no loss if *he's* dead," says Nutter, as Anders pushes the wire gate open and the two of them advance into the Mortlake gloom. Their torch beams skid across the rusted deck. "*If* he's dead. . ."

"Young Smiff was not lying," says Anders. He knows that boys like Smiff have no love for the police. Whatever happened here this evening must have been bad indeed to send him running to Airdock Green for help.

It doesn't take them long to find the bodies. They are lying just where Smiff said; Big Norm Trendlebeare and Spicy Rick, two of Mulligan's mates. Blood has spread in lakes upon the rust around them. Both are missing their right hands. Anders goes to the nearby hole in the deck and shines his torch down. Snow eddies in the beam, dancing in the complicated breeze between the city's wheels. Costa Mulligan hangs in the nets where Smiff left him, a fat fly in a rusty spider web.

"There must have been more than one killer,"

Nutter says. "These were big lads. To take all three down. . . Must have been a bunch of them."

"But the hands," says Anders, feeling queasy and trying not to let it show. All these years a policeman and the sight of blood can still do that to him. "Why take their hands?"

"As a warning," says Nutter. "To rival gangs."

"There are no rival gangs." Anders stoops to study a scrape mark on the deck. "Anyway, who'd see this warning? If Smiff hadn't chanced to be here it might have been weeks before we found these fellows."

Nutter says nothing. He's sulking.

"The boy said there was just one attacker," Anders reminds him.

"The boy was jumping down a hole at the time," says Nutter. "You can't take his word on any of it. For all we know he helped do in Mulligan and his cronies and then came scampering to us to get himself an alibi."

"He was frightened."

"He was actin'."

"Nobody is that good an actor."

Anders torch lights up bright scratches in the rust. He follows them into the mouth of an alley where shadows sleep among the hulks of huge, abandoned machines. Beside them, flower-shaped stains where blood has dripped. The sort of stains that Anders would expect to see if, say, someone carrying three freshly severed hands had run into that alleyway. But what about the scratches? Are they the marks of hobnailed shoes? Metal boots?

"You're too soft on these scavenger kids, Sarge," Nutter is saying, back at the alley's mouth. "Same with that girl I nabbed. Foreign mossie scum, and you talk to her like she's your long lost. . ."

"Quiet!" says Anders.

A few yards ahead, in the shadows beneath a huge old crane, he has spied the glint of moving metal.

4

Up, up the city climbs. Through gaps in the clouds the people on the higher tiers can see the lakes and rivers of the lowlands glinting in moonlit far behind. London has never climbed so high. There are parties to celebrate; the music of string quartets mingles with the steady howling of the wind. If London can conquer the Shatterlands, it can do anything.

At Airdock Green, Smiff sits sipping at the tea which Constable Pym has given him. He's calmer now, but not yet calm enough to face a night alone in his nest behind the starboard back-up heat exchangers on Tertiary Street. He sits and watches Pym, who is crouched in front of the station's big wooden filing cabinet, flicking through the papers inside. Through the spy-hole on the cell door the prisoner watches too, with her unreadable eyes.

"Here we go!" says Pym. He stands up with a sheaf of papers in his hands. Each week Airdock Green is sent a copy of all the police reports from other stations on Base Tier, badly typed on grey recycled paper. Constable Pym is the only one who bothers reading them. "I knew it reminded me of something," he says, waving the reports cheerfully at Smiff. "Listen. '*Friday 10th May. Body identified as Sid Simmonds, Track-Plate Cleaner*

3rd Class, recovered from no. 14 axle housing. Badly mangled; right hand missing.' They'd put it down as accidental. Thought he'd got caught in the machinery. And here's another, back in Sternstacks; right hand missing. And. . ." He sets the papers on the desk and leafs swiftly through them. "Disappearances. Eight . . . nine . . . ten of 'em this fortnight past. Ten men gone overboard, it seems. But did they fall, or were they pushed? And were they missing their right hands when they fell?"

"When I was a child," says a voice behind him, in surprisingly clear Anglish with a northern lilt, "I worked in the base tier of the city of Arkangel. One time we ate a little scavenger town. A nasty little place, but it didn't even bother to flee when Arkangel came swooping down on it, so it got eaten. Just thirty men aboard. All dead. All with their right hands missing. We found the hands heaped up in an old warehouse near the bows, like a nest of big white spiders."

"Blimey!" says Smiff, all saucer-eyed.

"D-don't listen to her, Smiff," warns Pym. "She's just tryin' to frighten us. Spreadin' panic and discontent, that's what they do, these Anti-Tractionists. I went on a course about them."

21

"You should be frightened, policeman," says the girl. "Your sergeant and the other one aren't coming back. I know what it is, that thing out there. It will kill them too, and take their hands.

5

"Who's there?' says Karl Anders, into the dark under the old crane. He hears Nutter's regulation-issue boots on the deck behind him and says without turning, "I don't

22

know why they don't just clear this district. The council's always nagging us to recycle everything. Why not recycle these old machines?"

"'Cos the Engineers are always talking about getting the Wombs working again," says Nutter wearily. "Good thing if they did, too. Trouble with this city is, we don't make anything any more. . ."

"Wait here," says Anders, before the constable gets started on some recycling of his own, rehashing some tirade from the news-sheets about how foreign imports are crippling London's industry. With his torch in one hand and his service revolver in the other he goes cautiously into the rattling, rust-scented dark.

"You'd best come quietly," he says to the shadows. "I'm armed."

Above his head big chains swing clanking, stirred by the city's movement. Nothing else moves. Nobody answers. His torch beam lights up strewn ducts and old papers under the rusting crane. It lights up a square pit in the deck where some other hunk of machinery was once attached.

The pit is full of hands.

"Great Goddess!" Anders starts to say, but

before he can get the words out a shadow moves. He starts to turn. Sees dark, oily robes, a hood with more shadows inside it and two . . . those can't really be green glowing eyes, can they? They must be goggles, reflecting a green light from somewhere. . .

A raised hands sprouts knives; not one, but four. Anders fumbles with the safety catch of his revolver. He hears himself say, "No!" Then the crash of Nutter's pistol deafens him. The robed attacker stumbles but does not fall. Nutter comes running and the pistol goes off again. The robed shape goes backwards and then up, bounding like an ape up the side of the crane, dropping into the darkness beyond.

"After him!" Anders yells.

They go round the crane. The robes flap under an arch ahead. They follow. Round a corner, through stacks of old crates. Each time they think they've lost the fugitive he's there again, a footfall ahead, robe tails vanishing around a corner.

Above the ceaseless voices of the wheels and engines comes a new sound; the snare-drum rattle of the little railway that runs through Mortlake, carrying solid fuel from the Gut to the old auxiliary Godshawk Engines near Sternstacks.

The line has been enclosed in a wire cage to stop men like Mulligan jumping aboard the unmanned trains and helping themselves to the fuel.

"He's trapped!" shouts Nutter.

The fugitive is running down a street which both men know is a dead end. The walls of the shuttered construction hangars tower up on either side, and the railway in its cage cuts across the end. Beyond the railway line lie brighter districts: Engine 12 and Ditch Street. The glow from their street lamps flickers through gaps between the trucks of the passing train. The fugitive is silhouetted against it, slowing as he reaches the fence and realizes the policemen have him trapped.

"He's tall. . ." says Anders.

The fugitive looks back at him, and again he catches that glint of green eyes. Then the fugitive goes through the fence. He reaches up with one hand and pulls the heavy mesh of the cage apart, tearing a hole that's big enough for even him to climb through.

"No!" says Nutter scornfully, as if his eyes expect him to believe something impossible.

Anders keeps running. The fugitive leaps aboard the last of the trucks as it trundles past.

Anders runs right to the fence and stops to take careful aim. In all his years as a policeman he's never yet shot anyone, but this seems like a good time to start. In another second the train will vanish through a tunnel beneath a big old metal building. He pulls the trigger and the gun jumps in his hand and he knows he's hit the figure squatting on the last truck because he sees a puff of smoke or dust or something spurt from its chest. But it doesn't fall; just turns and looks at him as the train carries it out of sight.

As the clatter of the wheels fades he hears footsteps behind him. Spins with the gun ready, but it's just Nutter, winded, running up behind. They stand there together, bracing themselves against the train cage as the city lurches under them, scrambling over some granite reef.

"It wasn't human," says Anders. "Bullets don't hurt it."

"Not human?" Nutter starts to chuckle, then realizes his chief's not joking. "What, then? A werewolf? A nightwight? Maybe we should be using silver bullets! We missed him, that's all."

"My shot hit all right. So did at least one of yours." Anders shakes his head, staring at the curve and gleam of the narrow tracks where they

26

plunge into that tunnel, trying to remember where they go. "It was a Stalker," he says.

"They're just in stories, aren't they?"

"Oh, they were real enough." The ghosts of long-ago history lessons stir in Anders's memory. There was this rusty head he liked to go and look at, in the Hammershoi Museum, when he was a lad. He says, "There was a culture once that knew how to resurrect the dead. Not their minds, just their bodies. Armoured them and sent them into battle, in the wars they used to have back in the days before Traction, when rival cities worked out their differences by fighting instead of just eating one another. The last of the Stalkers were supposed to have perished at the Battle of Three Dry Ships, but there's always been rumours of one or two survivors. Old things. Insane and dangerous."

"But how's one come to London?" asks Nutter, still not sure if he should take this seriously or not.

Anders shrugs. "Up from below, I suppose. London's been moving slow these past few weeks. A thing like that, if it was lurking in the high places, could have climbed aboard. Unless. . ." He turns suddenly, looking at Nutter. "It's no coincidence. This thing appears, and that girl you arrested, on the same night. There's a connection."

"What?"

"I don't know. Let's get back to Airdock Green and ask her."

6

"Sarge!" says Constable Pym excitedly, when the two of them get back to Airdock Green. But Anders goes straight past him to the cell, leaving Nutter to pour two mugs of tea, fortified with a good dash of something stronger from the bottle they keep for emergencies in the top drawer of the filing cabinet. Smiff, who seems to have appointed himself a sort of deputy constable for the night, fetches the official biscuit tin.

The girl stands up as Anders opens the cell door.

"She speaks Anglish, Sarge!" says Pym.

"Of course she does," says Anders. "*Everybody* speaks Anglish in the air-trade. And if she really doesn't we can get a translator in. But by the time I can get one here, her creature may have killed again."

Something changes behind the girl's eyes. She says, "It is not *my* creature."

"It arrived the same time you did. I think Corporal Nutter's right; you're some kind of saboteur and you've brought that thing aboard."

"No," says the girl.

"No," says Pym, behind him in the doorway. "That's what I was trying to tell you, Sarge. It's been here for days and days. A fortnight maybe. There's been deaths and disappearances."

Anders looks at him, then back at the girl.

"He's right," she says. "I tracked it here. It is very old and it has been wandering the world for a long time. I followed the stories, from city to city, settlement to settlement; stories of murders and missing right hands. In most of the places it's been, people don't even know what it is; they think it's a bogeyman, a hungry ghost. Aboard Murnau they called it Struwelpeter; on Manchester it's the Fingersmith. Most places, people just call it the

Collector. It takes the right hand of everyone it kills."

Some of the anger goes out of Anders. He sits down on the cell's hard bench. "Why?"

"Maybe it's planning to open a second-hand shop."

"Very funny, miss. But I meant, why did you trail it here?"

"Because I want it. You're right. I'm an Anti-Tractionist. I hate all mobile cities. But I'm not so stupid that I think I could blow them up with little fireworks like the one your man found on me." She shoots a look of scorn at Nutter. "If I had a Stalker to do my bidding, he could tear your city apart with his iron hands. He could kill you all one by one."

"But why would it do your bidding?" Anders asks. "Why wouldn't it just cut your throat for you, and take your pretty hand for a souvenir?"

The girl shrugs. "Nothing, maybe. But I've heard about this other Stalker, a bounty killer up in the northlands. Mister Shrike, he's called. Kills men and women without pity, for anyone who'll pay. But he won't harm children; the young, he takes pity on. I thought maybe the Collector would be the same. Maybe he'll listen to me. Maybe I can make him turn his talents to a good cause, and help me rid the world of these juggernauts of yours."

Anders ignores the notion that destroying whole cities full of people is a good cause. "It spared Smiff," he admits. "But you're older than Smiff. What, fifteen? Sixteen? Not a child. Maybe he won't take pity on you. . ." He laughs. "But you've already thought that through, haven't you! That's why you had the demolition charge with you!"

The girl tilts her sharp little chin at him, sensing mockery. "If I clamp it to his armour and let it off, not even a Stalker could withstand that."

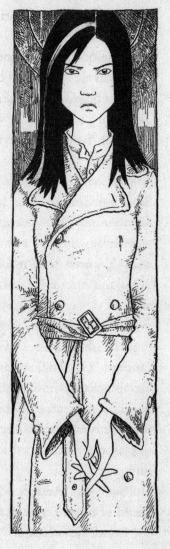

Anders shakes his head. "What's your name, girl?"

"Fang." She spits it at him.

"That's not a name," says Smiff.

"It might pass for a name among heathen Anti-Tractionist easterlings," Nutter admits grudgingly.

"Well, believe me, Miss Fang," says Anders, "I've met this Collector. If you were close enough to clamp things to its armour, you'd be dead." *Yet I'm not dead*, he thinks. *Why did it run when me and Nutter found it? A Stalker must know mere bullets couldn't pierce its hide. Unless. . .* "It doesn't know that it's a Stalker," he mutters. "Old and insane. . . And the hands. What's *that* about?"

"Why are we stood here listening to this mossie minx?" asks Nutter. "We need to be calling for support. This Stalker thing could be halfway to Sternstacks by now, murderin' as it goes. Send word up top, sarge. Get some of them lads from the Gut who think policing means posing about in plastic armour; let them help us deal with this thing."

"No," says Anders. "If we call for help the Guild of Engineers will hear of it."

"Good!" says Nutter. "They got death rays and

electric guns and all sorts stashed away in the Engineerium, I've heard."

"Exactly. So you can imagine how they'd love to get their hands on a working Stalker. Not to mention young Miss Fang here. I want to deal with this thing myself, if I can."

He leaves the cell door open as he goes back out into the office. Fang's demolition charge lies on his desk, neatly labelled as EVIDENCE in Constable Pym's boyish handwriting. He picks it up, weighing it in his hand and trying to imagine the blast it would create. Powerful enough to tear apart a town's deck plates, but focused. It seems to him that the girl has provided him with the perfect anti-Stalker weapon. If only he can get close enough to use it?

"Did you hear all that, Smiff?" he asks, meeting the wide eyes of the boy who sits beside the stove.

"Get him out of here, sarge," says Nutter. "He scoffed all our best biscuits."

"But we need him," says Anders. "You heard what Miss Fang said. These creatures are kindly to the young. That's me and you ruled out, and even Pym. Smiff here is the one we need to talk to it for us; lure it close, so I can pin this pretty medal on it." He holds up the demolition charge.

Smiff shakes his head. He keeps on shaking it while he slides down off his chair and backs away. He keeps backing away until the wall stops him. "I ain't going to go looking for that thing again, mister. I 'scaped it once, I might not get so lucky next time."

"But it won't harm a child. That's why it spared you last time. You'll be perfectly safe. Well, safe. Safeish."

Smiff just shakes his head some more. "You don't know that. You don't know nuffink. You just got *her* word on that, and she's not even a Londoner."

He points, which makes them all turn to look at Fang. She has emerged from the cell and stands behind them, listening. Nutter, when he sees her standing there, grabs her by her arm and says, "Get back in there, you—"

"Leave her," says Anders sternly. "We need her. The boy's right. We can't ask him to face this danger for us. Miss Fang can do it."

"What, you mean take *her* off to Sternstacks with us?" Nutter can't begin to mask his contempt. "Let her talk to this creature, and turn it against us? Or run off into the dark first chance she gets?"

By way of answer to the last point, Anders brings the handcuffs from his pocket and locks Fang's thin wrists together again. "If she runs, Nutter, you can shoot her. And if she says more than ten words to this Collector before I attach the charge to him, my name's not Karl Anders."

7

It's a funny thing, but now he knows what it is, Smiff can't get the Stalker out of his head. It's the biggest thing that's ever happened in his small life, that robed giant barging past him, pruning Costa's boys like weeds. It seems a pity not to get another look at it; a *proper* look like, before Sergeant Anders blows its mean old machine soul to the Sunless Country.

When they've gone, Anders and Nutter with

the girl between them, leaving Constable Pym to mind the shop, he sits a while longer by the station stove. Eyes the biscuit tin, but knows the nice ones are all gone. He sits and thinks about his Stalker, and wonders what it's doing now.

Constable Pym has his long nose in those filing drawers again. As soon as that girl said her name he knew he'd seen it somewhere. He flicks through the file marked S and soon finds what he's looking for. An alert issued nearly a year back, brought to London a month or so ago by some wandering aeronaut. *Anna Fang. Escaped Slave: Wanted for Theft of Money and Airship Parts by the Direktorate of Arkangel.* There's a grainy photograph of the girl, younger and acne-speckled, but that stripe of white hair is unmistakable.

Eager to share this latest breakthrough (his second in one night!) Pym turns to show the sheet to Smiff. "Hey, look at this! No wonder she hates Traction Cities!"

But Smiff is gone. The biscuit tin's gone with him.

8

It's a long way to Sternstacks, downhill along the dingy, steeply tilted streets that skirt the central Engine District, leading past the Engineers' great experimental prison at Piranesi Plaza. "That's where you're headed for," Nutter tells the girl with a leer. "All sorts of toys they've got in there for loosening Anti-Tractionist tongues. Literally, sometimes."

Luckily the streets are almost deserted. The only people they pass are harried engine-minders hurrying from one emergency to another, with no time to wonder where two policemen are going, or why the girl they have with them is handcuffed. They pass down Shallow Street, which isn't shallow at all tonight but canted at an angle that makes them shuffle and stagger like comedy drunks. At the street's end, litter that has slid down from higher districts near the city's prow has collected in drifts against the plinth of the statue of Charles Shallow himself, one of London's first and least-favourite Lord Mayors.

At Sternstacks they step out of the iron shadow of the tiers above into air that's cold and almost fresh. Fang tilts her face up hoping to see stars, but she's out of luck. All around her the huge exhaust stacks of the city rise, taller than any tower she's ever seen, some striped like garter snakes, some so fat that lesser stacks and flues twine round them like ivy round a giant tree. From their high snouts the smoke and smuts and filthy gas of all the city's engines fume, forming a cloud that blots out the sky.

"I found a whole parasite town up there in that lot once," says Nutter. "A little flying place called Kipperhawk. They'd anchored it to London's stern with hawsers and it was hanging in the smokestream, sieving out minerals and such. Cheeky cloots."

"It's a town-eat-town world," says Anders.

They walk past darkened offices and workshops to the place where the little railway track emerges from Mortlake. A line of trucks is being unloaded there by men in the orange jackets of the fuel corps, the fuel emptied into hoppers which will feed the ancient Godshawk engines which still stand here, too old and feeble to power London's usual travels, but still useful when there's a big push on. Anders goes over to the foreman. "Seen anyone come out of Mortlake tonight?"

"Mortlake?" The man looks at him like he's crazy. "What's up? Costa's boys causing trouble?" He peers past Anders, trying to ogle Fang through the ripple of hot air escaping from his engines. "Who's the girl?"

"Police business," says Anders.

"Suit yourself. But if you see my 'prentice on your travels, send him to me, would you? I haven't seen him since last tea break."

"It's here," says Anders, when he gets back to where Nutter and the girl are waiting. "An apprentice from that fuel gang has vanished. The Collector has collected himself another hand."

Even Fang has the decency to look a little nervous as they head sternwards. There is no one about. Walkways lead aft between huge horizontal ducts. The ducts steam, filling the air with mist. Smuts drifting down from above swirl in the mist like snow gone bad. Sometimes there's actual snow as well. By the time they get near to the high barriers at the stern, visibility is down to a few yards. Anders stumbles over the body of the fuel-team apprentice before he sees it. It lies where the collector left it, in a sticky dark puddle in the middle of the street.

"So much for your theory," Anders tells the girl. He takes out his handkerchief and spreads it over the dead boy's face. "He's younger than you, and your Stalker didn't show *him* any pity."

"What now then?' asks Nutter.

Men appear silently and all around; their rubber-soled shoes make no sound on the deck plates and their long, white rubber coats blend perfectly with the drifting steam. Four Engineers with pale bald scalps and the red cogwheel symbol of their Guild tattooed on their foreheads. Two carry sleek guns; a third is weighed down by something vaguely gunlike but so huge, and so encrusted with wires and coils and dials, that it's hard to tell.

"Is there a problem, sergeant?" asks the leader, a senior Guildsman, his eyes invisible behind faceted goggles.

Anders steps forward, half hoping that in the Sternstacks murk these newcomers won't notice Fang. But they *have* noticed her, of course; the eyes of the three gunmen are creeping all over her. He chooses his reply with care. The Guild of Engineers started out as London's mechanics and technicians, but on a mobile city mechanics and technicians are men of great importance, and over the centuries the Engineers have come to wield huge power. Upsetting them could end a man's career.

"Murder, sir," he says. "Three scavengers dead."

"And the girl?" asks the Engineer, goggles glittering like flies' eyes as he swings them towards Fang.

"A witness, sir, assisting us with our enquiries."

The goggles swing back to Anders. "These Scavengers. Were they mutilated?"

"Their right hands had been taken off, sir."

"Mmm," says the Engineer. Behind him the man with the big gun-thing shifts position, adjusting its weight. The others stand still as statues (which isn't very still on London's shuddery decks). Black smuts settle on their white coats; they are speckled like Dalmatians.

"You may return to your station," the Engineer says. "We have this situation under control. Your witness will remain with us."

From the corner of his eye Anders see Fang turn her face to look at him. She's wondering what he'll do. He's wondering the same thing

41

himself. It's a surprise when he hears himself say, "No."

The Engineer raises one well-pruned eyebrow.

"She's in my custody." says Anders. "For her own protection."

"You have questioned her?" asks the Engineer.

"Oh, we know about the Stalker, sir."

The Engineer doesn't so much as twitch a nostril. They must be great poker players, Anders thinks, if games of poker are permitted in that cheerless Engineerium of theirs. But his men start at that word, "Stalker".

"I didn't realize the Engineers knew about it, sir."

"The Guild of Engineers know everything," the Engineer snaps. "One of our survey teams encountered the creature known as the Collector three weeks ago, when London first entered these hills. We subdued it and brought it aboard. We were keeping it under observation in one of the old Wombs."

"Not keeping it under very *good* observation, were you?" splutters Nutter. "It's killed a dozen men on Base Tier. . ."

"That was part of the experiment," says the Engineer. "We wished to see how it behaved in the mobile-urban environment. London is no longer the largest or fastest city in the Great Hunting Ground. If we are to compete with the new megalopolises we may need to adjust our hunting strategies. If we could reproduce these Stalkers and insert them into the engine districts of prey cities they could prove useful. However, this Stalker has proved less controllable than we had hoped. We have lost contact with the Engineers who we put into Mortlake to study it. It has been decided to shut down the experiment."

"That contraption will kill it?" asks Anders, pointing at the big gun-thing.

"It is already dead." The Engineer permits himself a cold smile. "As are you, sergeant. We cannot have mere policemen prying into the business of our Guild."

He steps aside. The two gunmen behind him raise their weapons. Anders tries to think of something to say and finds that he is empty of words. But before the Engineers can shoot, something comes trundling at them down the slope of the deck, a small thing, cylindrical, rattling and clanking as it rolls into the open space between Engineers and policemen.

"Bomb!" shouts a voice, out of the vapours and the swirling snow.

The Engineers stare at the thing just long enough for Anders to butt their chief aside and swing a punch at the nearest gunman. He grunts and goes backwards, crashing into the one with the giant Stalker-gun, which goes off, arcing blue lightning everywhere. In the jagged light of it Anders sees the girl Fang swing a high kick into the face of the second gunman, who drops his weapon as he falls. She doesn't see the leading Engineer stepping towards her from behind, drawing a shiny silver pistol. But Nutter does, and throws himself between girl and gun as it goes off.

Then Anders has the Engineer by his rubber collar. He wrenches the gun out of the man's hand. The fly's-eye goggles shatter as he drives his head against the nearest duct.

Something bumps against the toes of Anders's boot and he looks down and sees that it's the bomb. Only it isn't a bomb; it's the biscuit tin from Airdock Green police station. Smiff stands in the swirling steam, staring at the felled Engineers.

"I followed after you, Sarge," he says.

Anders finds that he's too shocked to say anything. The dazed Engineers are grovelling on the deck. He kicks their guns away and goes to Nutter, who's crouched by a duct, hand pressed to the wound in his shoulder. Fang stands watching him. "He saved me," she says. "Why'd he do that?"

Nutter groans, looking like he wonders the same thing.

"Because you're a human being and so's he," says Anders, moving Nutter's hand and studying the wound. "Also, it's his job."

"Blimey," says Nutter, his face pale grey, tears running down it.

"You'll be all right," Anders promises him, although he's not sure how, because even if he can get Nutter patched up there's going to be trouble coming down on them for assaulting an Engineer Security Team. "Come on. . ."

9

He heaves Nutter up, yells for Fang and Smiff to follow and sets off up the deck's steep slope, all thought of hunting the Collector gone, starting the long walk back to Airdock Green. They've gone ten paces when he hears a voice behind shout, "After them!", and a bullet flicks past him and spangs off a stanchion. He wishes he'd hidden those men's guns better, or brought them with him, or thought to hit them harder. It occurs to him, as he pulls Nutter into the feeble shelter of an alleyway, that he should perhaps have killed them.

Nutter has fainted. Anders lays him down, says to Fang, "Take care of him," and quickly undoes her handcuffs. Then he creeps back to the alley's end. There's an old shrine there to Sooty Piet, the god of the Engine District. Ander's crouches behind it and peers out between the beer bottles and sheafs of lucky money that have been propped against the plinth as offerings.

The Engineers are making their way towards him, leaning forward like mountaineers as London heaves itself up a steep ridge and the slope of the street grows more extreme. There are five of them, and for a moment Anders wonders where the fifth one came from, before he realizes that the one at the back is far too tall to be an Engineer, and that his eyes are stabbing rods of green light through the mist.

"Watch out!" he shouts. He can't help himself. He'd leap out into his hunters' path to warn them of the threat, but Smiff has crept behind the shrine with him, and holds him back.

"No, sarge!"

One of the Engineers shrieks as the Stalker scythes him down. The others turn. The giant gun-thing goes off again, scrawling its blue lightning all over the Stalker, but it seems the Engineers have miscalculated; the current doesn't seem to bother him. The electricity wraps around him like tinsel round a Quirkemas Tree as he cuts down two other Engineers and then finally turns his attention to the one who's shooting him, reaching through the lightning to wrench the big gun apart, and its operator too.

Smiff tries to pull Anders away, but the policeman can't help himself. He keeps watching as the Stalker sets about its work, quickly and carefully removing the right hand of each dead Engineer. Silhouetted in the backlit steam, its spiky outline and jerky movements make it look like a shadow puppet. It pulls back the sleeves of its robe, and Anders sees that while its left hand is a nightmare gauntlet of iron and blades, the right is missing; its arm ends at the wrist in a jutting metal prong and a tangle of rusty wires.

Carefully the Stalker takes one of the freshly severed hands and shoves it on to the stump. The fingers jerk. Anders imagines electricity flowing into the hand, filling it like a glove. The Stalker raises it up in front of its face, into the light of those witch-green headlamp eyes. It turns the new hand this way and that, considering. Then it tears it off, throws it aside, and reaches for another.

"Is *that* what this is about?" whispers Anders.

He's talking to himself. He doesn't even realize that he's spoken aloud until the thing turns its huge head towards him and the beams of its eyes come groping for him through the vapours.

How could it have heard him, over all the noise of London? But it has.

It puts down the hand it's holding and comes towards the shrine. Anders knows there's no escape for him. The best he can hope for is to buy some time so that the others can escape. "Run!" he tells Smiff, and stands to meet the Collector.

As he steps out in front of it, Fang's knapsack nudges his hip like a reminder.

"Is that what this is all about?" he asks.

The Stalker is very close. It moves slowly, as if perhaps the Engineers' lightning did it some damage after all. Its head is half helmet, half skull. From the helmet part long tubes and cables trail, plugged into ports on the armour which Anders sees gleaming under its torn and ragged robes. The skull parts are thinly papered with old skin. The lamps that are its eyes flare slightly as he asks his question. It stops and stands there in front of him, braced against the rolling of the deck, bladed hand half raised. Maybe it isn't used to being talked to. In all its years of hunting and killing probably nobody's said anything to it more interesting than "Aaaargh!"

"So you lost a hand, and so now you're looking for another?" says Anders. "Trying and trying to find a replacement. But you never can, can you? They're always too big or too small or too hairy or the wrong colour. So you keep on searching. . ."

The Stalker twitches its head and the eyes flicker. "*Must . . . repair. . .*" it says. Its teeth are metal. Its voice rasps through them like a rusty file.

"Repair?" Anders fights the urge to look to his right, down the alley, to see if his companions have escaped. *How many years?* he thinks. *How many hands?* His own right hand is busy in Fang's knapsack, fingering the smooth curve of the demolition charge. He keeps talking. "You need to adapt, my friend. People lose hands and arms and legs and all sorts of things, but they learn to live without them. I lost my whole family; my wife and daughter, killed when London ate our town. That was worse than losing a hand. But I adapted, see?"

The Stalker has lost interest. "*Repair,*" it says, and its head tilts downwards, looking to size up

Anders's hand. Feeling in the knapsack, he turns the switches on the demolition charge; safety off, then the detonator. He remembers, as he draws the charge out, that he has no idea how long the fuse is set for.

"Here," he says.

The Stalker doesn't seem to know what the charge is. It doesn't seem to care. It watches Anders's hand as he reaches out and lets the charge's magnets clamp it to its armour, through its robes. Anders can guess what it's thinking. *Is this the right one at last? Is this finally the new hand I need?* And he surprises himself with a thought of his own: *Poor old thing.*

But he's not hanging about to let it try his mitt for size. As soon as its clawed gauntlet starts to reach for him he turns and runs, glancing back just once. The Collector is lumbering after him, the demolition charge pinned to its robes like a tacky brooch with one red light on it, red as a ruby.

He doesn't hear the explosion. There is only his sudden running shadow, flung on the deck plates in front of him. Then something hits him in the back like Sooty Piet's shovel. He feels the sorts of sensations that fools pay good money for in fairgrounds. Time gets stretched out, and when it finally gets a grip on itself Anders learns that the demolition charge has not just destroyed the Collector, it has blown a big, roughly circular hole in the deck plate. Through this hole gravity and the steep slope of the deck are dragging him. He claws for a grip at its raggedy edge. He hangs there by his slowly slipping fingertips, grunting as they strain with the effort of supporting his whole heavy policeman's body.

He looks down. In the light that spills past him through the hole he can see bits of the Collector strewn in the net beneath the city. A hand; a blank-eyed head. The body, or whatever was left of it, is gone. Presumably that's what tore the immense hole in the net, right under Anders's dangling size nines.

His fingertips slip another eighth of an inch closer to the edge of the hole. He says a quick prayer to Peripatetia, the goddess of mobile cities, in whom he does not really believe.

Like an answer, a small voice from above says, "Sarge?"

Smiff is looking down at him over the edges of the hole. His small hands sieze Anders's right wrist and tug, trying uselessly to haul him up. Anders is afraid that if the boy doesn't let go, they'll fall together. "Go!' he says. "Fetch help!" Knowing that he'll be long gone before Smiff can bring any help to this remote portion of the deck. *Unless Fang or Nutter are still around. But Nutter's too badly hurt to help, and Fang will be far away by now if she has any sense. . .*

Then, just as the hand Smiff's clinging to loses its grip entirely, strong fingers grip his other wrist, and there she is, her pretty face quite ugly with the effort as she strains to heave him up. And somehow, between them, her and Smiff, they do it; like snow-mad fishermen landing a walrus through a hole in the ice, they drag him up and lie there beside him, gasping, panting, laughing with relief on the hot deck, listening to the shouts and footsteps of the approaching emergency crews.

10

Afterwards, when Nutter has been taken off to the infirmary and they are all back at Airdock Green, she tells him, "I heard what you said to the Collector. About your wife and daughter."

Anders is studying the list Pym made of her airship's cargo, and the "wanted" note from Arkangel which he has paperclipped to it.

Fang says, "My father once docked our airship on a little ice-town, to wait out a storm. But in the storm's heart great Arkangel came and ate the town, and we were caught, and set to work as slaves aboard Arkangel. They treat slaves hard there. My parents. . . All that kept me alive was knowing that one day I would escape, and I would destroy Traction Cities."

Anders says, "With me, it was a silly accident. The town I lived on, it was pretty, but it wasn't well-built. Some of the tier supports gave way when London ate it, and Lise and Minna were caught in the collapse." He looks up from the grainy photo on the "wanted" note to her real face, across his desk. "You can't fight cities on your own, you know. If that's your ambition, you should go to Shan Guo, Kerala, Zagwa. The lands of the Anti-Traction League. They have armies and air-fleets to keep cities at bay. At least you wouldn't be on your own."

Fang says, "I thought I was your prisoner, policeman."

Anders carefully tears the papers in half, and then in half again, and again. He drops the pieces into the red recycling bin under his desk. "It's been a busy night," he says with a yawn, "and I still haven't got round to filing a report on you."

Fang watches him with those dark, dark eyes of hers. After a while she says, "You can come with me if you like. You can join the Anti-Traction League too."

"Me?" Anders chuckles. "Why would I do that? I'm a townie through and through."

"But London killed your family!"

"It was an accident."

"An accident caused by this stupid system, this insane, evil system, this Municipal Darwinism that makes city chase city. . ."

Her voice grows shrill and scratchy. How wonderful it must feel, thinks Anders, to be so young, so angry and so certain that you're right.

"I have work to do here," he says gently. "I don't know if it was a good idea of Quirke's to start cities moving all those years ago, but I do know there are plenty of good people aboard London, and somebody has to protect them from the bad ones. This is my city."

"But. . ."

Anders yawns and swings his chair around to face away from her. "Goddess, but I'm tired! Do you know, if a prisoner chose to make a break for freedom now, I don't think I could do a thing about it."

There is a long silence behind him. Then he hears her footsteps cross the room, and the sound of the door opening. He feels the breath of engine-scented air as it swings slowly shut. He is alone.

He gives her ten minutes, then goes outside. The motion of the city has changed; it's no longer climbing. Smiff and Constable Pym are walking towards him from the direction of the hospital on Crumb Street. He greets them.

"Corporal Nutter is going to be all right," says Smiff.

"And what about the girl?" asks Pym.

"Girl?" Anders looks blankly at him. "I'll teach you something about good police work, Constable: don't let yourself get distracted by unimportant details. Concentrate on the big picture. Which at this present moment means going inside and starting to work out how we can report last night's events to the Council of Guilds without mentioning mysterious girls or disagreements with Engineers."

"Yes, sarge," says Pym, saluting smartly.

"What about me, sarge?" asks Smiff, lifting his grubby face.

"You can go with him," Anders says. "I'm sure Pym can find some work for you. We'll be short-handed around Airdock Green till Corporal Nutter's fit for duty again. Who knows, there might even be enough money in the petty-cash tin to pay you, once we've bought a new biscuit tin."

They leave him. He walks on alone to the air dock and out along one of the quays into the grey, cool, early morning air at the edge of the city. The little red airship has gone from her berth. He looks up to see if he can catch a glimpse of her flying away, but cloud wraps the Shatterhorns. He'll not see Anna Fang again. He grabs hold of the handrail at the quay's end to steady himself and stands there in the cold, clean wind. London is tilting forward now, starting down the southern slopes. All the things which had slid to the back of the city on its way up will now be sliding forward again. The girl was right, thinks Anders; it is a strange way to live. But he knows no other.

The clouds ahead of London thin and part. The sun is coming up over the plains of Italia. The daylight gleams on lakes and rivers and slow, fat, unsuspecting towns.

THE WORLD OF MORTAL ENGINES

One of the greatest fantasy worlds
ever created. Read them all...

FEVER CRUMB

Thousands of years from now, a baby is abandoned in the
ruins of London. Rescued by some eccentric Engineers, Fever
Crumb grows up unaware that she is the keeper of an explosive
secret. Are the mysterious powers she possesses the key that
will save London from a new and terrible enemy?

A WEB OF AIR

In a faraway corner of a ruined world, a mysterious boy is
building a flying machine. Birds help him, and so does a
beautiful, brilliant engineer called Fever Crumb. Powerful
enemies stalk them — either to possess their fantastic
invention, or to destroy the secrets of flight forever.

SCRIVENER'S MOON

(Coming in April 2011)

In a future land once known as Britain, nomad tribes are prepar-
ing to fight a terrifying enemy - the first-ever traction city. In
the chaotic weeks before battle begins, Fever Crumb must jour-
ney to the wastelands of the North in search of a mysterious
black pyramid, whose secrets will change her world forever.

MORTAL ENGINES

Many centuries after the terrifying traction cities were created,
London is on the attack. In the violent chase, Tom Natsworthy is
flung from the speeding city with a murderous scar-faced girl.
They must run for their lives – and face a terrifying new weapon
that threatens the future of the world.

PREDATOR'S GOLD

The city of Anchorage is accelerating across the Ice Wastes, and
when Tom and Hester's tiny airship is attacked by rocket-firing
gunships, the ice city offers sanctuary. But it is no safe refuge.
Devastated by plague and haunted by ghosts, Anchorage is
heading for the Dead Continent.

INFERNAL DEVICES

Wren's parents, Tom and Hester, are happy living in static
Anchorage, whose rusting engines are long dead. Yet their
daughter is desperate to escape – and a charming submarine
pirate is ready to help her. But the object that she steals from
him ignites a conflict that will tear the whole world apart…

A DARKLING PLAIN

London is now a radioactive ruin whose hunting days are over.
But the predator city hides an awesome secret that could bring
an end to war. Tom and Wren risk their lives in its dark under-
belly, and, alone and far away, Hester faces a fanatical enemy who
possesses the weapons and the will to destroy the human race.

www.mortalengines.co.uk

© Judith Weik

Chris Priestley is the author of the chilling and brilliant *Tales of Terror* series and the haunting novel *The Dead of Winter*. He is also a talented artist. His illustrations and cartoons have been published in many national newspapers and magazines, including the *Independent* and the *Economist*. Chris lives in Cambridge, where he continues to write his seriously scary stories. To find out more about Chris, visit:

www.chrispriestley.blogspot.com

NEW FROM
THE MASTER OF THE MACABRE

Can a monster and a boy ever really be friends?

Find out in this fantastically frightening gothic novel

TERRIFYING READERS FROM
JUNE 2011

THE TEACHER'S TALES OF TERROR

CHRIS PRIESTLEY

BLOOMSBURY

LONDON BERLIN NEW YORK SYDNEY

For storytellers everywhere

Bloomsbury Publishing, London, Berlin, New York and Sydney

First published in Great Britain in March 2011
by Bloomsbury Publishing Plc
36 Soho Square, London, W1D 3QY

A CIP catalogue record of this book is
available from the British Library

ISBN 978 0 9566276 9 8

Typeset by Hewer Text UK Ltd, Edinburgh
Printed in Great Britain by Clays Ltd, St Ives Plc, Bungay, Suffolk

1 3 5 7 9 10 8 6 4 2

www.talesofterror.co.uk
www.bloomsbury.com

1

MR MUNRO

It was the beginning of March and the air was chill and dank. Mrs Nesbitt, the head teacher of St Apollonia's School, stood in the playground, peering up at the darkening sky through her wire-rimmed spectacles. She shivered and hoped that the snow that was forecast would not arrive.

St Apollonia's was marking World Book Day by having a special celebration of the school's Victorian heritage. All of the staff and pupils had been asked to dress up for the occasion and, in the main, the pupils – or at least their parents – had made a reasonable effort.

The snow would spoil the formal group photographs that were going to be taken in the playground that afternoon. There was a lovely old class photograph in the office from the 1890s and Mrs Nesbitt thought it might be nice to have similar ones done of each of the present year groups with their teachers.

Turning away from the glowering sky, she was somewhat startled to see a strange man standing in front of her. She had not heard his footsteps at all. It was as if he had materialised out of the cold air itself.

He was tall and thin, his face pallid and sour, with a large expanse of forehead beneath a sharply receding hairline. He wore a dark three-piece suit, and a watch chain twinkled across his waistcoat. He had the air of a butler about him, thought Mrs Nesbitt – or an undertaker, perhaps.

'You requested a supply teacher,' he said after a moment, seeing the confusion on her face.

'Ah – Mr Munnings?' she said. 'Of course.'

'Munro,' he said, correcting her. 'It is Mr Munro.'

'Oh – I'm terribly sorry,' she replied. There seemed something strangely familiar about him. 'Have you worked at St Apollonia's before?'

'Many years ago, yes,' he replied, looking across the tarmac to the school entrance.

His tone of voice gave the distinct impression that his previous experience of the place had not been a joyful one. Though looking at his cheerless expression, she doubted whether many of his experiences were joyful.

'It was very good of you to make yourself available at such short notice,' said Mrs Nesbitt. 'I'm afraid Mr Filbert has been taken ill. He was so looking forward to today. It's such a shame.'

Mrs Nesbitt looked at Mr Munro's clothing and smiled.

'And thank you so much for taking the trouble to get into the spirit of our Victorian Day. Your suit is very . . . very *authentic*.'

Mr Munro raised an eyebrow and let it fall slowly before speaking again.

'Where should I go?' he said.

'You are with 7UM, Mr Munro,' she replied. 'They are a lively bunch.'

'Indeed?' said Mr Munro with more than a hint of disapproval.

'What lessons do you have planned?' asked Mrs Nesbitt.

Mr Munro held up a rather battered old leather briefcase.

'I shall be reading them some stories,' he said.

'Oh lovely,' said Mrs Nesbitt. 'Can I ask you what you've chosen?'

Mr Munro tapped his briefcase.

'I have brought a volume of Victorian short stories. I hope they may find them diverting.'

Mrs Nesbitt laughed.

'*Might find them diverting,*' she repeated. 'Oh, that's very good. You really have got into the swing of it. But what sort of stories are they? As I say, they're a lovely group – *lovely* – but they're likely to become a wee bit restless if –'

'I think these stories will be sufficient to keep them quiet,' said Mr Munro.

Mrs Nesbitt forced a smile. She did not like being interrupted and in any case she was not sure that the exercise was about keeping the class 'quiet'. She was about to point this out when her secretary came pattering towards them down the steps of the school.

'Mrs Nesbitt,' she said breathlessly. 'Sorry to disturb you, but there has been a bit of an incident.'

'What sort of incident, Mrs Jackson?'

'It's Luke Driscoll,' she said. 'He's brought a spear into school – a real spear. He says it's authentically Victorian because his grandfather's grandfather took it from a Zulu warrior and –'

'I'm so sorry, Mr Munro,' she said. 'But I must deal with this, I'm afraid.'

'Of course,' said Mr Munro. 'I quite understand.'

Mr Munro's mouth curved into a half smile. Mrs Nesbitt pursed her lips and narrowed her eyes. She suspected that Mr Munro was being somewhat less than supportive.

'Your classroom is through the main entrance, past the hall and the first on the right,' she said curtly. 'A teaching assistant should be with the class. They are expecting you.'

Mrs Nesbitt and her secretary trotted away up the steps, leaving Mr Munro standing alone outside the school.

The jagged spikes along the spine of the school roof and the sharp spire of its bell tower were silhouetted against the leaden clouds. A graveyard chapel could not have looked more sombre. Mr Munro raised his eyebrow once again, and walked slowly towards the entrance.

He could hear the sound of lessons coming from the classrooms as he walked past. The tiled walls and parquet flooring of the corridors reflected his passage as he strode soundlessly by.

Once he had reached the classroom in which he was to teach, Mr Munro stopped. Through the window in

4

the door he could see the pupils, all dressed in their Victorian costumes. They were, as Mrs Nesbitt had promised, a 'lively bunch'. And there was no sign of the classroom assistant. *No matter*, he thought.

Mr Munro turned the door handle and walked into the room. The children were still chattering when he seemed to appear in front of them like a thin, dark column of smoke. Some of them did not even register his presence until their neighbours nudged and pointed.

Mr Munro opened his briefcase, took out a book and slammed it down on the table with such force that it felt as though a shock wave had been sent through the room. A cloud of dust swirled around him.

'Good morning,' he said. 'My name is Mr Munro.'

A stony silence followed this announcement.

'I said,' repeated Mr Munro loudly, 'good morning, class!'

'Good morning, sir,' came the response.

''Morning, sir,' added a girl near the back a few seconds behind everyone else. A rosy-cheeked boy at the front giggled.

Mr Munro lurched towards the boy as a snake might towards its prey. The movement was so swift and so alarming that the boy nearly fell from his seat. Mr Munro placed his long fingers on the desk and leaned towards him.

'Are we to be enemies, boy?' he said, fixing the boy with his cobra stare.

'No, sir,' said the boy nervously. 'I don't think so, sir.'

'Good,' said Mr Munro, narrowing his eyes and studying the boy's face intently. 'That is very good indeed.

Because you do not want me as an enemy. Do you understand?'

This last question was directed to the entire class and – almost in unison – they replied, 'Yes, sir.'

Mr Munro smiled. 'Jolly good,' he said.

Mr Munro looked about the room. A great deal of effort had gone into making the room look like a Victorian classroom. There was a print of Queen Victoria, and another of Dr Livingstone. There was a yellowing globe and a map of the Empire. All it had needed was the right teacher to complete the picture. Mr Munro held up the book to the class.

'I thought that I might read you some stories today,' said Mr Munro.

There was a weak groan from someone in the second row of desks. Mr Munro silenced it with a glare.

'You do not like stories?' he asked.

'What sort of stories are they?' said a curly-haired boy near the front.

Mr Munro said nothing. He merely stared at the boy. It took several seconds before the boy realised what Mr Munro was waiting for.

'Sir,' said the boy belatedly.

Mr Munro smiled.

'They are stories of a rather macabre nature,' said Mr Munro with an odd grin. 'I have a taste for such tales.'

A girl put her hand up.

'Do you mean they are scary, sir?' she asked.

'Yes,' said Mr Munro. 'At least I hope you will find them so. But if you do not like "scary" stories I'm sure

we could find something else to do instead. Do you enjoy spelling tests, perhaps?'

'Oh, I love scary stories, sir,' she replied. 'We all do, don't we?'

The entire class eagerly and noisily confirmed this until Mr Munro raised his hands for calm. He opened his book and took out the leather bookmark.

'What's the story going to be about, sir?' asked a tall girl with glasses.

'It would rather spoil it if I told you, would it not?' said Mr Munro. 'But it will do no harm to introduce it, I suppose.'

He replaced the leather bookmark between the pages and closed the book once more.

'Have any of you by any chance been to the coastal town of Whitby in Yorkshire?'

A wall of blank expressions greeted this question and Mr Munro paused a moment or two before speaking again.

'It is a rather marvellous place in its way,' he continued. 'A picturesque fishing port with a romantic ruin of an abbey on the cliff top. It is famous for the Synod of Whitby, of course.'

It was clear by the blank faces that the fame of the Synod of Whitby had yet to reach St Apollonia's School.

'It is also famous for its whaling industry, for its fossils and for its jet. You know what jet is, I trust?'

'Yes, sir,' said a girl with her hair in plaits. 'It's a shiny black stone they make jewellery out of. My mother has a –'

'That is correct,' said Mr Munro. 'Of course, Whitby is also famous as the place where Count Dracula first came ashore in the sensationalist novel that bears his name.'

'Is the story about Dracula, sir?' asked a boy at the back.

'No,' said Mr Munro.

'Is it about vampires?' asked another boy excitedly.

'No,' said Mr Munro.

'Is it –'

'It is about *jet*,' said Mr Munro. 'In a way, at least.'

A wall of silent but palpable disappointment greeted this statement.

'It might be better if I were simply to read the story,' said Mr Munro.

He opened the book at the marked page, gave a searching look around the classroom to ensure that everyone was settled, and then began.

2

THE JET BROOCH

A small bell pinged shrilly as Martha opened the door. It was a dull and sunless day, but even so the tiny shop seemed gloomy and cave-like in comparison.

Martha Thriplow was still occupied with trying to recall the nightmare that had disturbed her sleep. She had barely noticed anything on her walk up from the harbour. It was something terrible, she remembered. But that was all she could remember.

Martha, her mother and her brother, Vernon, had been in Whitby for three days now and so far the holiday, such as it was, had been a joyless affair.

Martha's father had died almost six months previously and they had been dressed in black ever since. Their mother had promised that Martha and her brother might each have a piece of jet jewellery as a memento of this holiday. Martha was to have a brooch, Vernon a pair of cufflinks.

Martha had loved her father dearly. He had been so unlike the fathers of most of her friends. He had been kind and sweet-natured. He had taken a genuine interest in what she was doing. She missed him terribly.

9

But still she longed to have some colour in her life again. A piece of scarlet ribbon would have been enough. And she knew her father would not have disapproved.

The shop bell did momentarily rouse Martha from her melancholy mood, but it quickly returned when she remembered that they were shopping for jet – black, black jet.

The sunless little shop was jammed with cabinets and those cabinets were in turn crammed with jet jewellery of all sizes and designs. But it was as though they were in a jewellery shop for undertakers.

The whole point of jewellery was to sparkle and delight, thought Martha. It was meant to be pretty. It was meant to be frivolous and divine, not morbid.

This jewellery, on the other hand, was more like a collection of dead beetles. A funereal display of black brooches, earrings, hatpins and necklaces glimmered darkly from dusty cabinets.

At one end of the room there was a counter behind which stood a plump man whose face was baby smooth. He patted his chubby, pink fingers together and said, 'Good morning,' as they entered the shop.

Martha's mother bowed in reply and the man asked if there was anything he could assist her with.

'Cufflinks!' said Vernon excitedly.

The man eased himself out from behind the counter and showed Mrs Thriplow and her son a selection of cufflinks in a nearby cabinet. Martha sighed ostentatiously but was ignored.

Reluctantly she gazed about the shop, rocking back and forth, heel to toe. She thought she may as well pick

out something not too ghastly so that she could be ready when her mother asked and thereby curtail the boredom of this tiresome expedition.

A cabinet stood only a foot away and Martha peered in with a sour expression, as though she was looking at a bucket full of cockroaches. To her surprise, her attention was immediately taken by a large brooch.

Whereas all the other jet pieces in the shop windows of the town were either plain or horribly ornate, this piece was quite the strangest thing she had ever seen. The shopkeeper was hovering in attendance as Martha's mother pointed out another pair of grotesque cufflinks.

Martha leaned towards the case and squinted at the brooch. Suddenly the shopkeeper was at her side.

'May I be of some assistance, miss?' he asked, making her jump.

'Oh,' she said. 'Erm – yes. Could I have a look at that brooch?' Martha pointed to the brooch that had caught her eye.

Martha's mother bristled. She disapproved of her daughter taking the initiative – a trait she blamed on the indulgence of her dear departed husband.

'Of course,' said the shopkeeper with a thin smile. 'Let me unlock that cabinet for you.'

The man took a bunch of keys from his waistcoat pocket.

'It's that one,' said Martha. 'Do you see? The one with the sort of circle on it.'

'Ah,' said the man. 'A very interesting piece indeed. You have a good eye, young lady.'

Martha was unused to flattery and blushed immediately. Vernon giggled. Their mother sniffed disapprovingly. She knew what 'interesting' meant: it meant expensive.

The man tried several keys before he eventually found the right one and opened the door. The hinges creaked so much that Martha thought she must be the first person who had ever asked for it to be opened.

The shopkeeper reached in and picked up the piece, and held his gloved hand out to Martha. Freed from the dusty cabinet, the brooch seemed to glisten like a raven's eye.

'It's a lovely thing, is it not?' said the shopkeeper.

'Oh, yes,' said Martha. 'Isn't it, Mother?'

Martha's mother leaned over and peered down her long nose. Vernon sighed and made a great play of looking bored whilst waiting for his turn.

'What about my cufflinks, Mama?' whined Vernon plaintively.

'It is a curious design,' said Mrs Thriplow. 'I can't say I care for it.'

'It is a snake,' said Martha, taking up the brooch and studying it. 'Do you see, Mother? It's a snake eating its own tail.'

Mrs Thriplow's expression made it quite clear that this did not make the object any more attractive to her.

'That is correct,' said the man approvingly. 'It is called a uroboros.'

'Urob—' began Martha.

'It is an ancient symbol of the cyclical nature of the universe, of infinity, of eternity.'

'Oh,' said Martha.

'Heathen nonsense,' snorted her mother.

'Quite,' said the shopkeeper with a bow.

'Heathen,' repeated Vernon disapprovingly.

Martha turned the brooch over in her hands.

'Ow!' she said. The pin had pricked her finger. A tiny bead of blood twinkled on her fingertip.

'Yes,' said the shopkeeper. 'That is rather sharp, I'm afraid.'

'Please may I have it, Mother?' asked Martha, using the unnaturally sweet voice she saved for such occasions.

'Certainly not,' said Mrs Thriplow with a sniff.

'But I thought we were to have a souvenir of our holiday, Mother. I could wear it in remembrance of Papa,' said Martha.

'I hardly think –'

'But, Mother,' persisted Martha, her voice trembling a little as she sucked at the blood on her finger. 'Don't you see how perfect it is? It reminds me of the cufflinks Father used to wear.'

Mrs Thriplow looked puzzled. Martha stifled a sob.

'Yes – you remember,' she said. 'The snake's head ones.'

Mrs Thriplow did remember those cufflinks. They were ghastly and she seldom let her husband wear them. It had often been a struggle taming his vulgar tendencies when it came to cufflinks and tiepins. She would certainly not be allowing any such outlandishness in her son's choice of adornment.

'I suppose there is a vague similarity . . .'

Martha burst into pitiful sobbing.

13

'Martha, really,' said her mother. 'I do wish you might find some way of restraining these outbursts. If it really means that much to you, I suppose –'

'Oh, thank you, Mama,' said Martha, from behind a large handkerchief.

The handkerchief was lowered as soon as Martha's mother went to the counter to pay. Martha smiled. Vernon scowled. Martha frowned threateningly and Vernon backed away.

'What about my cufflinks?' asked Vernon as his mother put her money away.

'I think I've spent quite enough money for one day,' she said, looking at the shopkeeper. 'Good afternoon.'

'Good afternoon, madam,' he replied. He bowed to Martha as she left. 'Good afternoon, miss.'

Once they were outside, Martha held the brooch up and inspected it properly. It looked so different in the daylight. The highlights glistened in the sunshine but, if anything, the blackness of the jet seemed even deeper, even blacker.

She had not appreciated how detailed the carving was on the snake as it curved its way round the brooch: each scale was painstakingly inscribed and the face – particularly the needle-sharp fangs and the cruel eyes – was astonishingly lifelike.

Martha pinned her new brooch to the collar of her coat and the family continued on their way up the narrow lane to the long flight of stone steps that led to the church and abbey on the cliff top.

'It's not fair,' said Vernon once they were ahead and out of earshot of their mother.

'Life isn't fair,' said Martha, looking at her brooch.

'Anyway, it's horrible,' said Vernon.

'What would you know?' said Martha.

'I know something's horrible when I see it,' he said.

'So do I,' she replied, glowering at him.

Brother and sister glared at each other until their mother puffed up the last of the steps to stand beside them.

'Come along,' she panted. 'Come along.'

The Thriplow family explored the abbey ruins and visited the church of St Mary with its odd, ship-like interior. Then they walked among the rows of eroded, salt-scarred headstones of the graveyard.

Martha was fascinated by the way some of the graves seemed to be plunging right over the cliff, as the wind and tides gnawed at its foundations. Would the church tip into the sea one day, she wondered. Or the abbey? Nothing stayed the same. Everything changed. She looked at her black-clad mother peering at a headstone.

'Why does everything have to change?' she said. She looked down at her brooch and had an urge to take it off and hurl it into the sea. She missed her father terribly all of a sudden. She blinked and a tear trickled down her cheek.

The family returned to their hotel on the opposite side of the bay and ate their supper in near silence. They retired early, and even Martha's outrage at having to share a bedroom with her brother did not get its usual outing. She was simply too tired. She was asleep in an instant.

*　　*　　*

When Martha reached for her coat to look at the jet brooch the following morning, she found instead only the silver backplate and pin it had been attached to. Her surprise was replaced by anger almost immediately.

Martha strode over to her brother's bed and shook him roughly awake.

'What?' said her brother sleepily. 'What's the matter? What –'

'You know exactly what's the matter, you horrid little sneak!' said Martha. 'What have you done to my brooch?'

'Your brooch?' said Vernon. 'I haven't touched your silly brooch. It's ugly and vile and I wouldn't touch it for all the world.'

Martha slapped him across the face.

'Liar!' she hissed.

'I shall tell Mother!' said Vernon, holding his face.

'Of course you will, you little weasel,' said Martha. 'You always do!'

Martha's mother had been passing their door and walked in to find Martha looming threateningly over her brother.

'Martha!' she hissed, having the foresight to close the door behind her in case another guest might happen by. 'What is the meaning of this?'

'He has taken my brooch,' she said. 'He's broken it and stolen it!'

'Martha, control yourself!' said Mrs Thriplow. 'Is this true, Vernon? Have you taken the brooch?'

'No,' wailed Vernon. 'And she slapped me!'

Mrs Thriplow closed her eyes and took a deep breath.

'Do be quiet, Vernon,' she said. 'What will the other guests think? Martha you will not strike your brother. Do you understand?'

'But –'

'Enough!' their mother commanded, clapping her hands together. 'I expect the brooch has simply fallen off somewhere in the room. Have you even looked?'

Martha was forced to admit that she had not.

A thorough search was undertaken but no brooch was found. To make matters worse, when asked by her mother, Martha was unable to say, without any doubt, that the brooch had been intact when they arrived back at the hotel after their walk.

Martha had been so tired she had taken her coat off without registering whether the brooch was still in one piece.

Mrs Thriplow explained the situation to the hotel manager and the hotel staff were quizzed without much success until another guest overheard and said that she had seen Martha arrive back and had noticed that the brooch seemed to be broken. She had been about to say something at the time, but her husband had called her away.

Martha was forced to croak a begrudging apology to her brother for wrongly accusing him. Mrs Thriplow puffed herself up into a state of outrage about shoddy craftsmanship.

'We shall go back to that shop this very morning!' she declared. 'We shall demand that he replace that brooch forthwith.'

Mrs Thriplow had seen an opportunity to make her daughter come away with a more suitable piece of jewellery. Martha sighed and pushed her chair back from the table noisily.

'I don't want another brooch, Mother,' said Martha. 'That was the only thing in that horrid shop that was not vile.'

'Nonsense!' said Mrs Thriplow.

'Could I look at the cufflinks, Mother?' asked Vernon.

'I don't want to go back there,' said Martha grumpily.

'They have no right to sell shoddy goods, Martha,' she replied. 'It is precisely because so few people return and complain that these people continue to behave so abominably. I blame you, Martha.

'I was on the point of leaving but you would insist on my buying you that frightful brooch. I knew there was something suspect about that awful man. Well, he will rue the day he decided to try to swindle Cornelia Thriplow!'

And so the Thriplow family left their hotel and walked down the steep hill to the harbour and over the bridge. Fishing boats were returning as they made their way through the market and up through the narrow lanes.

Near to where the long flight of stone steps leading to the church began, Martha and her family stopped and stood staring in confusion at the window of a haberdasher's.

They retraced their steps and came back to the same spot. They walked on a little and then returned, all with the same bemused expression.

'But that's impossible,' said Vernon, giving voice to a sentiment shared by his mother and sister.

For though they were all sure that they should be looking at the window of the jet shop where they had bought Martha's brooch, there was no sign of that shop at all. That is – there was a shop there, but it was the aforementioned haberdasher's, not a jet shop.

Martha's mother went to the door of the shop and opened it. All three of them peered in. Even if it was possible that the jet shop had packed up its business and been replaced by this one in such a short space of time, the haberdasher's shop was a completely different size and layout. The door opened the opposite way for one thing. The Thriplow family retreated to the other side of the street.

Mrs Thriplow was a practical, unromantic sort of a person and was ill-prepared to deal with such strangeness so soon after breakfast. She felt a migraine rolling in like a storm.

'How is that possible?' said Martha. 'The shop was here. And now it's not.'

'Don't be silly, dear,' said her mother. 'We must be mistaken.'

'But –'

'*We must be mistaken, Martha,*' Mrs Thriplow repeated fiercely and was already walking back down the hill, eager to be away from the dizzying illogicality of that place.

Martha and Vernon followed her after a moment's hesitation, each of them looking back over their shoulders at the place where the shop should have been but was not.

*   *   *

The subject of the shop that was not there was avoided at supper. Mrs Thriplow had refused to speak of it again, and Martha and Vernon had not had any opportunity to speak of it while alone. By the time they went to their room they had both privately veered towards their mother's way of thinking. They must have been mistaken about the location. It was the only answer.

Martha got changed hurriedly, as she always did, whilst Vernon was in the bathroom. When she put on her nightdress, she noticed a bloodstain on it, just below her neck.

She wanted to get a better look. The only mirror she had in the bedroom was a small hand mirror and that was really not much use. Something about the shape of the stain made her realise that it corresponded to where she would have worn her brooch. She had pricked her finger on the pin. Had she done the same when she had put it on her coat?

She unbuttoned the front of her nightdress, nervously checking that Vernon was still in the bathroom. Pulling the nightdress aside, she was horrified to see that there was a small hole in her flesh, as if an arrow had pierced it. Surely it was much too large to have been made with a brooch pin?

Then Martha felt something move under her nightdress and jumped back, shrieking and slapping herself, trying to catch whatever it was and bat it away. Vernon came in and was very much amused by his sister's curious antics.

Until she turned to face him.

Vernon's face was transformed in an instant from mirth to horror as he shouted out, pointing and staggering backwards. Vernon ran for the bedroom door and flung it open, throwing himself through, screaming for his mother.

Martha felt something moving across her face and put her hand up to flick it away, but it was not *on* her face she now realised – it was *underneath*. It was under her skin.

Martha knew instantly and instinctively that it was the snake from the brooch – what did the man call it? – the uroboros. It was somehow inside her flesh, slithering round her eye socket and across her forehead. She looked in the mirror and screamed.

Martha Thriplow awoke with a gasp, sitting upright in her bed, the bedcovers strewn on the floor. She was bathed in sweat and her heart was hammering.

'Martha?' called Vernon.

Martha made no reply. She patted herself all over for a sign of the thing under her flesh but could feel nothing.

Whilst Vernon gazed on in bafflement, she grabbed the mirror and pulled her nightdress aside. Martha saw with relief that the hole in her chest was gone. It had been a nightmare, she thought. Just a nightmare.

Martha Thriplow ate her breakfast with all the relish of a reprieved felon who had escaped the axeman's block. She even shrugged off Vernon's teasing of her behaviour on waking.

Martha's nightmare had been so shocking that she had no inclination to revisit it in her thoughts, and

with startling speed a fog seemed to roll over and obscure it entirely in her mind, much to her relief.

By the time Mrs Thriplow had gathered her children together for yet another shopping expedition into town, Martha was back to her normal self.

They made their way down the hill from the hotel, crossed the bridge and then walked along the stone jetty to the little lighthouse at the end. Mrs Thriplow encouraged them to take large breaths of the sea air as she always did, convinced as she was of its efficacious properties.

As they strolled back along the harbour wall, Martha remembered that she had woken from a nightmare, but she could no longer recall what it had been about. She found this unaccountably irritating and her mood was not improved when her mother announced that they were going to shop for some pieces of jet jewellery as suitably sombre mementos of their stay.

A small bell pinged shrilly as Martha opened the door. It was a dull and sunless day, but even so the tiny shop seemed gloomy and cave-like in comparison.

Martha Thriplow was still occupied with trying to recall the nightmare that had disturbed her sleep. She had barely noticed anything on her walk up from the harbour. It was something terrible, she remembered. But that was all she could remember.

Mr Munro snapped the book shut as he finished the story, making most of the class jump in the air. A girl

22

near the back let out a small whimper. Mr Munro smiled.

'There,' he said quietly. 'I trust that was not too dull for you?'

Looking down at his desk, he noticed the name 'Montague' carved into the wood in a neat copperplate script and mused for a moment on the falling standards in graffiti.

'Are you going to tell us another story, sir?' said a boy at the front.

Mr Munro looked up and raised an eyebrow.

'Would you *like* another story?' said Mr Munro.

'Yes please!'

Mr Munro opened the book and began to look through it.

'Ah, yes,' he said. 'I think you will enjoy this one.'

'Is *this* one about Dracula, sir?' said one of the boys eagerly.

'None of the stories are about Dracula,' replied Mr Munro.

A prim-looking girl near the front put her hand in the air.

'Or vampires,' said Mr Munro.

The hand went down.

'What is it called, sir?' asked another girl.

'It is called "Simon Magus",' said Mr Munro, opening the book and taking out the leather bookmark, 'and concerns a boy called Simon and a holiday he took with his guardian to the glorious city of Siena in Tuscany.'

3

SIMON MAGUS

Simon had enjoyed much of his visit to Italy. He had particularly appreciated the chaotic energy of Rome and had been utterly entranced by tales of Christians being thrown to lions in the Colosseum.

He had thrilled to the stories of gladiators hacking away at each other in front of a bloodthirsty crowd.

He had enjoyed eating out in the crowded piazzas with their huge fountains. Rome was loud and raucous and just a little bit dangerous.

And in Florence they had witnessed a fatal stabbing in the Piazza della Signoria. Blood had spurted out of the dead man's mouth. A woman had fainted. It had been the most exciting thing Simon had ever seen.

But Simon was not enjoying Siena. The only interesting thing about Siena seemed to be that there was a dangerous horse race round the town square every year. Sadly the next race would not be run for months.

Simon's parents had both been killed in a ballooning accident in the Atlas Mountains of North Africa two years previously whilst he was away at school. He was in Italy with Uncle Henry, his guardian.

Uncle Henry had enjoyed a misspent youth and, like many who have been led astray in their younger days, he was determined that Simon would not replicate what he now saw as appalling errors of judgement.

Uncle Henry was very keen that Simon should embrace the arts and culture of Italy, but more importantly, fully engage with his Roman Catholic faith – a faith that had given Henry such solace in the years since the death of his beloved wife.

Their marriage had been childless, but possibly because of it, they had been everything to each other. It did mean, however, that Uncle Henry's knowledge of children was hazy in most respects.

His avuncular advice often took the form of warnings against the lures of Satan. Simon was rather intrigued by what these lures might be, but Uncle Henry was always frustratingly vague in that regard.

'Satan is everywhere,' his uncle had said.

'What does he look like?' asked Simon.

'Just like an ordinary man,' said Uncle Henry.

'Then how will I know if it's Satan?'

'Oh, you'll know,' said his uncle solemnly. 'Be on your guard. He is among us at all times, my boy. Waiting: waiting for his chance to ensnare a good boy like you.'

Simon was not a good boy, however. He had never been a good boy. But Uncle Henry meant well and Simon was very fond of him. When his guardian smiled down at him, he did his best to stifle a yawn and smile back.

They were in the Museo dell'Opera del Duomo. It held the treasures of the *duomo* — the cathedral — of Siena. He and Uncle Henry had just been in the cathedral and had lit candles – Simon for his parents and Henry for his late wife.

Simon had rather liked the cathedral. It had a sort of gloomy grandeur about it. But the museum was less to his taste.

It was not that it did not contain some interesting things. It was just that there were only so many statues and paintings Simon was prepared to look at in one day.

It might not have been quite so bad had Uncle Henry and Simon simply walked around on their own. Uncle Henry had quite a skill for bringing out the gory and unsavoury details that many guidebooks missed. He was particularly strong on the torture and grisly martyrdom of the saints. His description of the slow grilling of St Lawrence over an open fire was something that would stay with Simon for ever.

But, possibly aware of this dubious trait in his personality, Uncle Henry had decided that it might be better if they joined an organised tour group for their visit to the museum.

Their guide to the treasures therein was an Italian woman in her late forties who had the reddest lips Simon had ever seen.

'This is another exquisite tempera panel by Duccio and it shows a fascinating incident in the life of St Peter,' said the guide. 'Can anyone guess what it depicts?'

Simon had not the faintest idea and even less interest, but just as he was drifting off to thoughts of

battling gladiators, he heard his name mentioned and instinctively looked up.

'That is correct,' said the guide, pointing to a small painting. 'This figure here is Simon Magus. It is said that he had a dispute with St Peter in Rome. Perhaps some of you have already been to Rome?'

There was a murmur of assent from many of the assembled tourists, including Simon and his uncle.

'St Peter and the magician had a kind of a competition. Simon Magus wanted to show that he had the greater powers, so he built a wooden tower and climbed to the very top. The painting shows him levitating, held aloft by demons.'

Simon could see the little bat-winged figures beneath the magician. He had noticed these demonic figures in many paintings on their tour. They were often scratched and defaced in frescoes as if the faithful were trying to erase evil from their lives by erasing it from the paintings. But here they were untouched.

Simon Magus was standing triumphantly in the sky, arms outstretched. *How wonderful*, thought Simon. *How wonderful to be able to fly.*

'But St Peter prayed to God for assistance,' continued the guide, 'and the demons supporting Simon Magus were exorcised. Without their Satanic assistance, the magician fell to his death. Here,' she said, pointing to another panel, 'we see him on the ground.'

The guide crossed herself at the end of this story.

'It is not a common theme in religious painting,' continued the guide. 'There is a painting by Filippino

Lippi for instance — and another by Gozzoli . . . But it is not a common subject.'

Simon peered at the painting.

'I'm called Simon too,' he said as if in an effort to explain his interest. The guide nodded.

'St Peter was also called Simon, of course,' she said, 'before Our Lord gave him the name of Peter – the Rock.'

But Simon was far more interested in the flying Simon Magus than he was in the pious Simon Peter.

'Would you like to have a closer look?' asked the guide, heartened by Simon's interest. 'I have a magnifying glass.'

'Yes please,' said Simon.

Simon's uncle smiled approvingly as his nephew took the magnifying glass from the guide.

'You enjoy yourself, my boy,' said his uncle. 'I see someone I need to talk to.'

Simon nodded and watched with a wry smile as his uncle went over to talk to a woman they had met at the hotel the previous evening. His uncle had blushed boyishly when they had been introduced. It had been most amusing to watch.

Simon stared at the painting, passing the lens over the paintwork. He looked at the wooden tower and the figure of Simon Magus held above it.

He looked with particular relish at the winged demons that raised him up. They were spiky, shadowy figures; featureless silhouettes apart from their staring eyes, red tongues and white teeth.

He looked at the image of the fallen figure, face down on the ground, blood spattered around the head

like a red halo. It was all painted with a grisly attention to detail that Simon found fascinating.

But as he moved the magnifying glass across the painting, he became intrigued by another figure. Standing in front of St Peter in the section of the painting that showed Simon Magus and Peter arguing, was a man who stared straight out of the picture.

Simon could not believe his eyes. He had seen that man before – and here in Siena! He and his uncle had, the previous evening, eaten at one of the many restaurants in the Campo – the rounded piazza at the heart of the town where the horse race was held.

It had been an indifferent meal and Uncle Henry had gone to complain about the bill, and it was then that Simon had become aware of a man sitting nearby, peering off towards the cathedral with a strange self-satisfied expression.

Just before his uncle returned the man had turned and looked directly at Simon. It was a very unnerving thing to have that same face stare out of a painting, horribly enlarged by the magnifying glass. The guide leaned in next to Simon.

'It is quite a face, is it not?' said the guide. 'Such evil!'

Simon had to agree. The face bore an expression of arrogance and cruelty. The eyes were deep-set but piercing, the cheekbones high and the nose long and proud. A thin beard traced itself along his jaw and round his thin lips.

A woman in their party asked if she might take a look and Simon passed her the magnifying glass.

29

'Who is it meant to be?' said Simon, still struggling to make sense of what he was seeing.

'Nobody knows for sure,' said the guide. 'There are theories, of course.'

The guide dropped her voice and leaned close to Simon's ear.

'Some say that it is a portrait of Satan himself,' she said and crossed herself again.

Simon looked back at the painting and at the cruel face staring out at him.

'Satan?' he said, his throat very dry all of a sudden. Simon turned to see if his uncle was returning. He felt the colour draining from his face.

The guide marshalled her group and they began to move off across the room to an open doorway.

Simon was dazed. 'Satan is everywhere,' he remembered Uncle Henry saying. '*Everywhere.*' Simon looked for his uncle again but could not see him anywhere. He walked in the direction he felt his uncle must have taken, but stopped in his tracks, haunted by that cruel face.

He happened to look back towards the painting and saw that, now that the tour group had moved on, a man was standing examining it with great concentration.

Even before the man turned to face him, Simon knew it was him. It was the man from the painting – the man who was staring out; it was the man the guide had said was thought to be Satan.

The man looked at Simon, who stared back at him in disbelief. Simon looked from him to the painting and

back again and the man seemed to follow his gaze. Then the same cruel expression he wore in the picture appeared on his face.

'Simon?' It was Uncle Henry. 'Are you all right, my boy? You look as if you've seen a –'

'That man . . .' said Simon, pointing.

But there was no one there.

'What man, Simon?' said Uncle Henry.

Simon looked around, peering into the clusters of tourists dotted around, but there was no one even vaguely familiar.

'Nothing, Uncle,' he said quietly. 'I thought I saw someone I recognised.'

'Well,' said Uncle Henry, putting his arm round Simon. 'What say we go and look at the view, eh? Get away from these fusty old masters. You look as though you could do with a swig of fresh air.'

Uncle Henry had mentioned the panorama at breakfast and after a steep climb, Simon and his uncle eventually reached the roof of the museum. Simon had been in a daze most of the climb and was jolted out of it by the bright sunlight hitting his face.

There was a low wall to their right and a magnificent view out across the terracotta rooftops of Siena, the bell tower rising above the Palazzo Pubblico, the rolling hills of Tuscany beyond. Simon began to feel a little calmer. Some people, he knew, hated heights, but Simon loved being high up. It made him feel more alive.

And in this case it also seemed to clear his head. Up there, under a bright blue sky, he seemed less convinced

31

of what he had seen and certainly less sure of its meaning.

Satan? In a museum, looking at paintings? Was that really very likely? There had to be some other explanation. He had allowed himself to be unnerved by Uncle Henry and his warnings. He had panicked. It was not at all like him. Simon now felt a little foolish.

'Bother,' said his uncle suddenly, looking at his watch. 'I have to go to the bank, Simon. I completely forgot.'

Simon smiled. More money from the bank meant more money for Simon to take when Uncle Henry had fallen asleep.

'If I don't go now, they'll shut up shop for one of their siestas,' continued Uncle Henry, 'and we'll have no money for lunch.'

'Must we go down now, Uncle?' said Simon. 'It's lovely up here.'

'I'll tell you what,' said his uncle. 'Why don't you stay here and enjoy the view?'

'Yes,' said Simon. 'I'd like that.'

'Shall we meet outside the bank in, say, half an hour?'

Simon agreed and his uncle disappeared through the doorway that led to the narrow staircase. Simon gazed across at the view. Two swallows whirled past, mouths agape, and as he turned to follow their flight, he saw that there was someone standing framed in the doorway.

For a moment he thought it was his uncle having returned with a change of plan, but as the figure moved

into the sunlight he saw that it was someone else entirely. Simon stared in horror and disbelief.

'No!' said Simon, staggering backwards.

'Calm,' said the man, putting up his hands. 'Calm, please.'

But Simon was anything but calm. 'You – you're in that painting,' spluttered Simon. 'How can you be in the painting and here? How?'

The man smiled.

'Calm yourself,' said the man. 'Please.'

'The guide said you are . . . that you are . . . S-S-Satan,' stuttered Simon.

'The guide is misinformed about many things,' said the man coolly.

'But that painting is hundreds of years old,' said Simon. 'How? How? You'd have to be a ghost.'

'I am a mortal man,' said the man with a smile. 'I assure you that I am no ghost. Nor Satan for that matter.'

'But –'

The man moved a little closer and dropped his voice.

'Will you listen to me?' said the man. 'And I will tell you how this happened. There is a logical explanation.'

'I want to go back,' said Simon. 'Let me go.'

'Let me explain first,' he replied in a tone that left no doubt that he would brook no argument.

'How?' said Simon, trying to work out the chances of getting past the man and through the doorway.

'Parts of the painting are many hundreds of years old,' said the man. 'And parts are not. Much is by Duccio. Some . . . is not.'

The man smiled crookedly and his deep-set eyes twinkled like water in a well.

'What do you mean?' said Simon.

The man took a deep breath and let it out slowly, looking out across the city.

'Look at this city, my young friend,' he said. 'This is my city. But they do not know me at all.'

'I don't understand,' said Simon.

'When Duccio painted his great altarpiece, it was carried to the cathedral in a torchlit procession. Can you imagine? Can you?'

Simon did not reply. The man indicated the whole city in a great sweep of his hand.

'What would it be like to be that famous?' he said. 'To be so loved? To have this whole city at your feet.'

'What has that to do with you?' said Simon. 'I want to go down.'

'Many years ago a Duccio panel came into the hands of my father,' said the man. 'He was the most skilled and trusted restorer in all of Tuscany – of all Italy, perhaps.

'It had been bequeathed to the city by an anonymous benefactor. The panel was damaged – badly damaged – and he had been asked by the Council of Siena to repair it so that it could be presented to the museum.

'But the truth was my father was not the craftsman he had been when young. His eyes were weak, his hand unsteady. More and more, he passed on the work to me – while still claiming credit, naturally.

'And so it was with the Duccio panel. And whilst I was engaged in its restoration my father became

seriously ill. As I continued the work on my own, a thought occurred to me.

'The notion that I might be able to pass my work off as that of the great Duccio began to obsess me. I knew the great man's work as well as anyone and I knew that I could match him. I would show my father. I would show them all!'

His eyes blazed as he said these words and Simon took a step back.

'There was a damaged section – the section showing figures next to Simon Magus when he meets St Peter. I decided that I would paint a self-portrait over that damaged section.

'Of course I was a fool,' he continued. 'If my father had died, my contribution would have been revealed. But he did not, and I was so caught up in this scheme I worked feverishly until it was completed.

'My own father's eyesight was so weak he did not even notice what I had done. He handed the panel over and the Council were delighted, of course. Days later my father died and I could not even attend the unveiling ceremony for fear that someone might recognise me and my crime.

'I moved away from Siena and found my true vocation in a life of forgery. It has been very lucrative. I am a wealthy man, my friend. But I had always wanted to return and see where it all began. It was a risk, of course, and now here we are . . .'

Simon's heart began to calm as he realised that he was in the company of a mere criminal. This strange man was nothing more than a forger.

'But do you see, my friend,' he said. 'If you tell people about this, then the panel will be seen as the forgery it is and taken out of the museum and I will be exposed as a trickster.'

'Why tell *me* about it then?' said Simon.

'You are a clever boy,' he replied. 'You would have told someone and suspicions may have been raised.

'But in truth, it feels good to tell someone. I was right. My work can pass as that of Duccio. I am his equal. And yet no one knows; no one but you, my young friend.'

The forger put his hands together as if in prayer and looked at Simon beseechingly.

'I beg you. I did not alter the Duccio for profit. No one has been harmed by the subterfuge. Can you find it in your heart to forget what you have seen? Will you give me your word that you will say nothing about these things?'

'Of course, sir,' he said. 'What difference does it make to me? You can forge as many silly paintings as you like as far as I'm concerned.'

The forger sighed with relief.

'*Grazie. Grazie*, my friend,' he said. 'Shall we shake on it?'

'Very well,' said Simon, holding out his hand.

The forger took Simon's hand and patted his arm with his other hand. Then he let his hand settle on Simon's arm and gripped it tightly.

'I truly wish I could trust your word,' he said forlornly. 'But I would be ruined if you did not keep it, you understand.'

And with that he gave a terrific heave on Simon's arm and Simon felt his feet leave the stone floor as his body sailed over the short wall of the parapet.

He felt himself hang momentarily in the air. Time seemed to come to a halt and he floated in space, the whole city stretched out below him like a map.

And then, with a horrible suddenness, the cobbled street seemed to hurtle upwards to meet his startled face.

→→·←←

Mr Munro peered over the top of his book.

'Please, sir,' said a moon-faced boy near the back of the class, holding up his hand excitedly.

'Yes?' said Mr Munro.

'I'm called Simon,' he said.

'How very interesting,' said Mr Munro uninterestedly.

He noticed some activity outside and walked to the window. Children were gathered together with their teacher for a group photograph. They had their backs to him and the photographer took the photograph just as Mr Munro looked out. He smiled at the thought of his face showing up at the window at the back of the picture.

He turned back to the class to find another boy with his hand up.

'Are you called Satan, perhaps?' said Mr Munro.

'No, sir,' said the boy. 'Richard, sir. My name's Richard.'

'And what can I do for you, Richard?'

'Can we have another story, sir?'

'*May* we have another story,' corrected Mr Munro. 'But I really don't think we will have the time.'

A wave of moans and sighs rolled towards the front of the class and Mr Munro pursed his lips, allowing himself a smile. He looked at his pocket watch and nodded.

'Perhaps just one more,' said Mr Munro.

The class cheered. Mr Munro raised his hands.

'That is quite enough of that, thank you,' he said.

The cheering promptly came to a halt. Mr Munro flicked back and forth through his book for a while until he finally placed his long finger on a page and nodded to himself.

'Yes,' he said. 'This one should do.'

'What is this story about, sir?' asked a girl at the front.

'What long hair you have,' said Mr Munro, ignoring her question.

The girl did indeed have a mane of long black hair that fell almost to her waist.

'Does your mother brush it for you?' he asked.

'Yes, sir,' she said. 'Every night. Otherwise it gets all tangled.'

Mr Munro smiled and nodded.

'I have a story about just such a mother and just such a lovely head of hair,' said Mr Munro. 'Would you like to hear it?'

The girl was very enthusiastic in her nodding. The boys nearby were less so.

'Excellent,' said Mr Munro.

4

LYDIA

Lady Overton brushed her daughter's long red hair. It was dark outside and the candlelight made the hair shimmer like fine strands of copper.

Tears began to well in Lady Overton's eyes as she looked out of the tall bay window, beyond her own pale reflection, towards the family mausoleum and the mighty cypress trees that stood behind it, silhouetted like wrought-iron spikes against the indigo sky.

For it was three months since poor Lydia had been laid to rest in that very tomb; three months since Lady Overton had said farewell to a precious daughter, and poor Eleanor had lost her beloved twin.

A full moon glimmered blindly, cataract white, hidden now and then by ragged clouds, and the wind that moved those clouds also shook the cypresses and rattled the window frames. A draught fluttered the candle flames and made the shadows shake and jitter.

Eleanor seemed to guess her mother's thoughts and smiled sweetly up at her in the reflection in the gilt-framed mirror that stood on the bedroom dressing table.

Lady Overton did her best to smile back. But her mind was aquiver with competing memories of her late daughter. Standing there, brush in hand, the pain seemed renewed and reinvigorated. The agony of loss is often waiting in the shadows of such mundane acts.

Every evening before bedtime, Lady Overton had come to her daughters' room to brush their hair. One hundred strokes every night, with the lovely brush backed with mother-of-pearl that had belonged to Lady Overton's grandmother.

Eleanor had endured this ritual because she knew her mother enjoyed it so, but she was without any great vanity about her appearance. Lydia on the other hand had been obsessive in this regard and in particular about her beautiful, long red hair.

Lady Overton had always told herself that she did not favour one girl above the other, but the truth was that she had always favoured Lydia. Eleanor knew it, and Lydia knew it.

To their mother, Lydia was like an angel come down to earth. This was, however, an act that Lydia had perfected for Lady Overton alone. To everyone else she was more devil than angel – and particularly to her poor sister.

It was Eleanor who was the real angel. She knew that her mother was not capable of thinking ill of Lydia and so saw no point in upsetting her mother with the truth about her wayward twin.

Despite the fact that Lydia showed her nothing but disdain and cruelty, Eleanor protected her sister and

covered for her, even on occasion taking the blame for some of her more unsavoury activities.

This kindness did not endear Eleanor to her sister. Far from it. Lydia despised her for what she saw as weakness and was happy to see sweet Eleanor ignored or chastised by their foolish, deluded mother.

But all this passed Lady Overton by. Or at least it did for many years.

Then one day she caught Lydia stealing from her – only the day after a servant had been dismissed for a number of petty thefts about the house.

Lydia had been caught red-handed, taking money from the locked box in which Lady Overton kept cash for household expenses – something Lydia did on a regular basis, having long since acquired a copy of her mother's key.

Suddenly a veil seemed to be pulled aside in Lady Overton's mind and Lydia's true character was now revealed in all its naked guile. Instead of begging her mother's forgiveness, Lydia simply began to giggle.

Lady Overton's world came tumbling down. She could say nothing. She turned from her daughter and walked briskly up the grand marble staircase heading for her room.

Lydia, seeing that the game was up, felt no further need to disguise her true nature. She followed her poor mother up the stairs, shouting one piece of foul abuse after another.

Lady Overton put her hands over her ears to try to block out the sound, but Lydia caught up with her mother and grabbed her arms to pull those hands away.

verton pushed her daughter aside. It was just
a push. But it was a violent one, powered by a savage
sense of disappointment and hurt.

There was a cry and a terrible succession of thuds,
each more sickening than the last. Lady Overton
turned to see her daughter at the foot of the marble
stairs, a pool of blood spreading out from beneath her
lovely hair.

'Help!' she cried. 'Oh God. Help!'

Servants came rushing out. Daisy, the under-parlour-
maid, dropped to the floor in a faint when she saw the
blood, cracking her own head open in the process.

The scene was utter chaos until Higgins, the butler,
arrived, and sent for the doctor. Lady Overton sat on
the top step in a state of shock, hugged by Eleanor.

It occurred to no one that Lydia had suffered
anything more than an accident. Everyone knew how
much Lady Overton doted on Lydia and no one could
have suspected her of any involvement in the girl's fall.
Lydia had not been popular among the servants and,
though none would have wished her dead, none
mourned her with any great conviction.

When Lady Overton finally came out of her daze, she
had managed to suppress the unpleasantness leading up
to her daughter's death and her own part in it, at least to
the watching world. At night, however, those moments
revisited her, clawing at her sleeping mind.

Lady Overton devoted herself to the funeral arrange-
ments and Lydia was laid to rest beside her ancestors
with all the gravitas the surviving Overton family
could muster.

A shrine to her memory was erected in the hall with an alabaster likeness on a small table and a vase which Lady Overton kept constantly stocked with freshly cut flowers.

Eleanor bore her mother's devotion to her dead twin sister with all the good-humoured fortitude she had shown when Lydia was alive.

She would have happily foregone the nightly ritual of the hair brushing, but she knew that – though her mother could never have voiced it – the exercise gave her mother a brief moment to imagine that Lydia was still alive and looking back from the gilded mirror.

And so it was that Lady Overton stood, half entranced by the repetitious action, her heart aching with a boundless melancholy. The sadness she felt at Lydia's death was tinged with a bitterness she could not acknowledge, a bitterness born of the revelation of Lydia's true character and her own part in her daughter's death.

The brush slid down the long red hair and it seemed to flow like liquid, like a long waterfall of red and gold.

Her daughter smiled at her from the mirror and Lady Overton smiled back, before looking out into the night once more, away to the resting place of her other daughter.

Lady Overton was startled to hear a piercing shriek. It was surely an owl, but it sounded so human. It was difficult to tell from which direction it came and there were owls all over the estate. But it did seem as though it came from the direction of the family mausoleum.

Lady Overton was sure she detected some movement in the blackness at the base of the trees, near to the wrought-iron entrance gate. She stopped brushing and peered into the darkness.

'Mother?' said her daughter. 'Is something the matter?'

Lady Overton looked back at the mirror and at Eleanor's concerned face.

'No,' she said. 'Of course not.'

She resumed her brushing. But moments later there was another shriek. She looked out of the window and this time there could be no doubt.

'Did you hear that?' she asked.

'What, Mother?' asked Eleanor.

'You heard nothing?' Lady Overton said with a frown.

'No, Mother,' she replied. 'What is it?'

'An owl,' said Lady Overton. 'I think I heard the old barn owl. You know what an unearthly din they make. You didn't hear it?'

'No, Mother,' said Eleanor.

'Never mind,' said Lady Overton. 'It was an owl. Nothing more.'

Lady Overton looked out of the window again and was alarmed by what she saw. There was something moving. Something – somebody – dressed in white was moving down the path towards the house.

Though it was dark, Lady Overton could see that the figure stopped occasionally to look back towards the trees, towards the family tomb, and then carried on towards the house.

The clouds parted and the opal moon shone weakly across the grounds. Lady Overton could see the figure clearly now. It made no sense and yet she could not doubt the evidence of her own eyes.

The stranger (it was a woman, surely – no, no, a young girl) looked up at the window at which Lady Overton stood, stopped and stared. Then she turned to run with great determination to the door of the house.

'Mother?' said her daughter again. 'What is the matter?'

'I don't know, my darling,' she said breathlessly. 'I thought I saw something outside . . .'

'Saw something?'

But whoever had been outside was now inside. Lady Overton had heard the door slam, and feet were pattering up the very marble stairs poor Lydia had tumbled down just months before. She could hear those same feet coming towards her along the hall. She could see the door handle move and the door slowly open.

'Oh my God,' she said, dropping the brush to the floor as the door creaked open. Her daughter walked in, her white gown edged with dampness. Lady Overton grabbed the back of Eleanor's chair for support.

'Mother,' said her daughter, standing in the doorway. 'Do you not know me?'

Lady Overton's grip on the chair tightened. She felt as though it was the only thing keeping her upright.

'Lydia!' said Lady Overton. 'God forgive me. I am so sorry. I did not mean to do it. It was an accident. I –'

'Please, Mother!' said her daughter. 'For pity's sake: Lydia is dead. I am Eleanor – Eleanor, Mother.'

Lady Overton seemed to struggle to take in this information and she blinked as though dazed. Eleanor? Eleanor?

'Something terrible has happened, Mother,' said Eleanor. 'I have sent Higgins to deal with it.'

Lady Overton turned and saw some figures running off towards the cypress trees, dissolving into the darkness as if consumed by it.

'Someone has broken into the crypt. Oh, Mother. Grave robbers! They have taken Lydia's body!'

'Lydia's body,' repeated her mother mechanically. 'Grave robbers.'

'Mother!' said Eleanor. 'Please. You must lie down – you must . . .'

Eleanor did not finish the sentence. She could see something reflected in the mirror. What was that behind her mother? There was something sitting on the chair. She moved to get a better view and gasped in horror.

'Mother!' she cried, putting her hand to her mouth and recoiling in horror. 'What have you done? What monstrous thing have you done?'

Lady Overton's mind seemed to have fogged and she was finding it unaccountably difficult to concentrate on what was happening. How could this be Eleanor, when she had been brushing Eleanor's hair the past half hour?

'Look at what you've done,' screamed Eleanor. 'Look at yourself!'

Eleanor ran from the room and Lady Overton looked at her hands as she reached out to call her back. They were covered in mud, her fingernails broken and bleeding. Her dress was likewise filthy and torn, stained with mould and laced with dusty cobwebs.

Slowly, slowly she turned to look in the dressing-table mirror. It was not Eleanor who looked back. It had never been Eleanor; she understood that now.

The face that stared back at her – if the word face could properly describe the grinning horror that lolled atop that shroud-covered corpse – was Lydia's.

Lady Overton remembered now: remembered how she had gone to the mausoleum in a madness born of grief and guilt; remembered how she had opened up the grave with her own bare hands and carried her daughter's rotting corpse to the place where it now sat, revealed for what it was, just as Lydia's true nature had been revealed before her death.

But Lady Overton's heart could not bear the weight of that dreadful recollection and struck its last beat as the clock in the room sounded the first stroke of midnight. She fell dead to the floor, a few strands of Lydia's long red hair still clenched between her fingers.

Mr Munro took a deep breath and surveyed the room full of upturned faces. How pale they seemed, he thought with satisfaction. A bell suddenly rang out and Mr Munro put his book down on the desk.

'Well,' he said. 'There we have it. I hope that you have not found the stories too disquieting.'

'Oh no, sir,' said a girl on the front row enthusiastically.

'I am very pleased to hear it,' said Mr Munro.

He put the book back in his briefcase, clapped his hands together and took a deep breath.

'Well, it was a pleasure to meet you all,' he said unconvincingly. 'Perhaps we shall meet again.'

'For more stories, sir?' said a boy.

'Perhaps,' said Mr Munro. 'Perhaps. Well – goodbye.'

'Goodbye, sir!' shouted the class in unison.

Mr Munro picked up his briefcase and, nodding to the class, he opened the door and walked out into the corridor.

The other pupils were milling about, changing classrooms and teachers. He winced at the noise of scraping chairs and loud voices. He would go to the office and find out which classroom he was in next.

'Mr Munnings?' said a voice behind him.

It was Mrs Nesbitt, the head teacher.

'Munro,' he corrected.

'Where have you been?' she said sternly.

'I'm not sure I appreciate your tone of voice,' he replied.

Two girls sniggered as they passed by.

'Well, I am very sorry to hear that,' said Mrs Nesbitt. 'But I'm afraid this is unacceptable.'

Mr Munro sighed.

'Is there a problem?' he asked. 'I realise my stories are quite challenging, but I find that most childr—'

'Mrs Mildew had to cover for you whilst you disappeared to wherever you disappeared to,' said Mrs Nesbitt. 'She was supposed to supervise the music hall rehearsals and –'

'Cover for me?' said Mr Munro. 'What on earth do you mean? I was with 7UM as you requested.'

Mrs Nesbitt took a deep breath.

'Look,' she said. 'I have no idea what you think you are trying to achieve by this nonsense. If you were not able to do the job, then why come to the school?'

'But, my dear woman –'

'I am not your dear woman,' said Mrs Nesbitt. 'I am not anyone's dear woman!'

'Really?' said Mr Munro. 'You do surprise me.'

'Very well,' said Mrs Nesbitt. 'If you were teaching 7UM, then I'm sure they will remember you.'

Mr Munro smiled.

'Oh – I'm *sure* they will.'

'Then let's go and ask them, shall we?' said Mrs Nesbitt. Mr Munro shook his head and followed her.

'Did you even bother to come into the school?' said Mrs Nesbitt.

'As I have already explained,' said Mr Munro with a sigh, 'I followed your instructions. I walked past the hall and went into the first classroom on the right and –'

'On the left,' corrected Mrs Nesbitt.

'Right,' said Mr Munro. 'You definitely said right.'

'I can't have done,' said Mrs Nesbitt.

'I assure you that you did,' said Mr Munro. 'And more to the point, perhaps that is the source of the

confusion. What I do not understand is that in my whole time teaching the class, no teacher came in. Who would have looked after those children had I not been there?'

Mrs Nesbitt had now come to a stop and was listening to Mr Munro's speech with the expression she was often wont to use on pupils when they made their excuses about missing homework.

'Could I ask you to just pop inside the classroom you say you were teaching in, Mr Munro?' she said.

There was something about Mrs Nesbitt's tone of voice that made him suspicious, but Mr Munro agreed and opened the door.

'I don't understand,' he said.

The room was filled with rows of desks, each with a computer on it.

'No,' said Mrs Nesbitt. 'Neither do I.'

'But I taught in this classroom not more than a few minutes ago,' he said. 'It had a blackboard, a globe over there. It was very convincingly decked out as a Victorian classroom. There was a map on the wall showing the British Empire . . .'

'This room hasn't been used as a classroom for years,' said Mrs Nesbitt. 'It is our IT room, as you can see.'

'But I don't –'

'I think it's best if you leave, Mr Munro,' said Mrs Nesbitt coldly.

Mr Munro stared at the classroom one last time and then walked into the hallway. In desperation he grabbed the door handle of the opposite classroom and opened the door.

But he knew he had not turned that way when he first walked to the classroom. Mrs Billings, the class teacher, looked concernedly at him, and the class stared until Mrs Nesbitt pulled him by the arm and coaxed him away.

'Mr Munro,' she said. 'I really must insist.'

Mr Munro nodded.

'Yes,' he said. 'Of course, of course.'

Mrs Nesbitt walked him to the office and said that she would have to make a formal complaint. Mr Munro nodded. She walked him all the way to the gates. She seemed eager to make sure he was off the property.

'Goodbye, Mr Munnings,' she said.

'Yes,' he said absent-mindedly, too distracted to correct her. 'Goodbye, goodbye.'

What a very peculiar man, thought Mrs Nesbitt to herself as she returned to her office. The Victorian class photograph caught her eye as she was checking her emails. She stood up and walked across, peering at the photograph.

'That's impossible,' she said to herself.

There in the photo, looking out of the window behind the children and their teachers, was the pale face of the man to whom she had just said goodbye.

Mr Munro decided to walk home rather than catch the bus. It was a long way but he felt that the fresh air might help. It didn't.

All the way home he thought about the classroom. In some thoughts it would be full of children, in others, full of computers.

'How?' he mumbled to himself. 'How could something like that happen? How could I be so wrong?'

An old lady who was walking past smiled benignly at him as if she saw a kindred muttering spirit. He scowled at her and quickened his step.

'You're exhausted,' he told himself. 'When was the last time you took a holiday? A proper holiday, I mean.'

He stopped and took a deep breath. Yes – that must be it. He had worked himself to a state of such exhaustion that he was actually seeing things. He would take some time off. Take a cottage in the country, perhaps?

Mr Munro decided to visit the library on his way home. He always felt comforted by the presence of books. He decided that some Romantic poetry might calm his mind and settled down at a desk with a collection of Keats.

After a while, he did feel a little better. The incident at the school still seemed horribly vivid though. Could he really have imagined those children? He shivered at the thought. Was this how madness began, he wondered.

Mr Munro called in at his favourite café and had a soothing cup of tea. Everything always felt better after a pot of Earl Grey.

But neither the tea, nor the poached egg he had with it, worked its magic today and though he tried to lose himself in The Times crossword, those children would insist on derailing his train of thought. He decided to give up and go home. An early night, that was what he needed.

It was already quite dark and there was a bitter chill in the air. Mr Munro was most of the way through the park and nearing the gates that opened on to the street where he lived when something made him stop and turn round.

Spittle-like snow was falling wetly. On the brow of the hill he had just crested was a ragged silhouette. It was only a group of children – presumably on their way home from school as he was – but for some reason he found them unnerving.

Mr Munro turned back towards his house and quickened his step. He had not walked more than a few paces when he felt the need to stop and turn round again.

To his horror he saw that the children were now only a few metres away and that these were not just any children – they were the very same children who could not have been in the computer suite.

Mr Munro could not look for more than a few seconds. He ran, clutching his briefcase to his chest, all the way to his front door and fumbled for his keys. He staggered inside and slammed the door, deadlocking it behind him.

He put his briefcase down on the hall table and went to the window to look out. The children were standing at the entrance to the park. The snow was falling more heavily now, the flakes lit by the street lamp. He gulped drily and pulled the curtains shut.

He turned on the television. For the first time in his life he watched a talent show, glad of the harmless inanity which drowned out all thought of the children for a while.

But only for a while.

Mr Munro glanced anxiously at the curtains and felt compelled to get up and confront his fears.

'They are imaginary,' he said to himself as he gripped the curtains. 'Imaginary. They are not there.'

He opened the curtains and let out a whimper. The children were clustered just outside the window staring in, their faces pale and wan in the streetlight. The girl with the long hair smiled at him, snow swirling round her like a flock of white moths.

Mr Munro shut the curtains again.

'You are not there!' he shouted. 'You are not there!'

He opened the curtains once more and the children were gone. A car drove past, but otherwise the street was empty. Mr Munro felt his heart lighten with relief and he clapped his hands together. He felt like Scrooge when the dreaded Ghost of Christmas Yet to Come becomes nothing more than his bed curtain.

'God bless us, everyone,' he said with a smile.

But he thought he would still take that holiday. A rest-cure was what he needed. A cottage. A cottage by the sea. Yes. The sea.

He was forced to acknowledge that he was clearly not a well man. He felt tired. His head hurt and he ached as though he had the flu.

Perhaps a holiday was not the thing at all. Perhaps he needed to be in a hospital – a place where his illness might properly be treated. The thought of ending up in such a place dampened his spirits, as he readied himself for bed.

He settled himself beneath the blankets and picked up the book that lay on his bedside table – *Tales of Mystery and Imagination* by Edgar Allan Poe – but immediately replaced it.

'Not tonight, I think,' he said to himself with a shudder as he leaned over and switched off the light and let the darkness embrace him.

And in that darkness, a voice spoke out, the speaker so close that Mr Munro could feel the chill breeze of their breath on his startled face.

'Please, sir,' it said, 'can we have another story?'

ANOTHER SPINE-TINGLING STORY
FROM CHRIS PRIESTLEY

THE
DEAD
OF
WINTER

CHRIS PRIESTLEY

BLOOMSBURY

'Deliciously creepy with lots of twists and turns'
Daily Mail

HAUNTING BOOKSHOPS NOW